TROUBLE
AT SECOND
BASE

Books by William R. Cox

FIVE WERE CHOSEN

GRIDIRON DUEL

THE WILD PITCH

TALL ON THE COURT

THIRD AND EIGHT TO GO

BIG LEAGUE ROOKIE

TROUBLE AT SECOND BASE

TROUBLE
AT SECOND
BASE

By

WILLIAM R. COX

DODD, MEAD & COMPANY
NEW YORK

Library of Congress Catalog Card Number: 66-12811

Printed in the United States of America
by The Haddon Craftsmen, Inc., Scranton, Penna.

U. S. 1448760

To Junior Keaton, a perfect model of a St. Bernard,
and to Eleanor, his proud and loving mama,
with continuing adoration

It was a clear and sunny day in Springtime, a Southern
California day, smogless, cheerful. The big dog ran across
the street at a busy intersection and everyone stared. The
light turned green and they still looked after him, until
the honking of horns drove them on into traffic.

His name was Junior. He weighed almost two hundred
pounds, although he had not yet reached his second birth-
day. He was light-colored and shaggy. He moved with the
speed and strength of the very young, tongue lolling, ears
flapping, nostrils wide and sniffing at the trail he imagined
he was following. Actually, he knew well enough where
he was going. He had been there in the family automobile
often enough.

He also knew that he was disobeying all the rules and
regulations laid down for Saint Bernard dogs by his family. He did not think of them as his owners, rather the
other way about, as those owned by him. However, he did

have a strong tribal feeling, which is why he was forging that afternoon toward the athletic field of Studio City High School, in the suburbs of the ancient and gigantic city of Los Angeles.

There was a small girl, not half his size, who stopped, squealed and reached out sticky hands. Her mother yanked her away, fearful, but Junior managed to get in a lick of his soft, warm tongue, tasting the chocolate which the child had been eating. He did not linger, although chocolate was high on his favorite dessert list. He kept going, directly down Curzon Street, toward his destination. There were many distractions, including a cat who hissed and made ready to fight, but Junior always tried to ignore feline behavior as feminine and irrational. His goal was the baseball field, and nothing could stop him.

He came to an intersection across which was painted in huge block letters, "SCHOOL ZONE—15 M.P.H." He could not read, but he new that this meant a certain safety was his if he kept his head up and paid attention to what was going on. He stood on the crosswalk, eyeing the cars going by.

Across the street was a high wire fence. Beyond it was an open area dotted with human forms. Junior's tail began to wag without command, quite of its own volition. He had come a good distance to reach this scene.

He looked right and left, saw his chance. He walked boldly and with some dignity between the white lines which led toward the promised land. He heard the sound of hard wood against smooth leather and emitted a short, happy bark. All was well in Dogland now. In a few moments he would join his personal, close friend and brother. Everyone would be pleased at his cleverness and good sense in this accomplishment.

He nosed along the fence until he came to a gate. There was, to his amazement, a barrier here. Someone had looped a small chain in a manner which prevented him from entering the enclosed field. He paused a moment, contemplating this.

He might jump over the gate, of course. He backed off and looked. He had suffered a sad experience sometime in the past when he had failed to clear such a wire barrier by a narrow margin. He decided against the leap. The fence was pretty high for a dog his size and weight.

Junior squinted through the wire. No one was paying any attention to him. The action was in the far corner of the enclosure. There were no girls around and about, he observed with satisfaction. He much preferred boys. They were all over the place. He had quite a time picking out the certain individual he had come so far to join. He whimpered a little. The gate was a nuisance. It was a circumstance upon which he had not counted.

He leaned a shoulder against the wire barrier. It moved, but it did not open.

He retreated a couple of steps and cocked his big head on one side. His left ear flopped up, giving him an unusual and undignified appearance. He was not worried about how he looked, however; he was worried about how he would get in there and join the proceedings.

He could see, now, that the game awaited him, needed him. It was a serious, concentrated contest. Without him, they would not be certain of which way to go, how to perform. He had spent hours upon hours, since he was no more than a muff of fur with stubby limbs and no jowls, yet, in learning this game.

Inside the Promised Land, Coach Charles "Chuck" Johnson was intent upon the field. He was a serious young man, with his dark hair crewcut beneath his jutting baseball cap. He had a strong jaw. His eyes were keen, his manner crisp. He was neither friendly nor unfriendly; he was judicial. He was trying to put together a team which would win the horsehide championship of Greater Los Angeles.

This was only his second year at Studio City High, in the San Fernando Valley, a part of the far-flung city school system. He was a very ambitious coach. He had been a player under Dedeaux of the University of Southern California, a student of the game rather than a great performer, a born teacher rather than a player. There were hundreds of would-be players in this vast school complex, but he had a comparative few to choose from. Nevertheless, he thought he had a chance to emerge with a championship.

One of the reasons for his confidence was now at bat. He was a tall, strong, big-armed lad named Harry Keel, a senior who had proved himself a fair-enough first baseman last year and whose bat was quick. On first base, by virtue of a walk, was Jack Pilgrim, another giant of a lad, who could also run and play center field. He was another reason for hopes of a roseate future for good, new Studio City High.

This was Chuck's tentative first team at bat. Harry Keel was his cleanup man, and strong Joe Simpson would come up behind him, another long-ball hitter. That made three of them in a row, counting Jack Pilgrim, already on first and taking his lead, hoping Keel would knock him around.

Coach Johnson lined them up for a practice game this way. He put his first-team battery on the Yannigans and his lesser pitcher and catcher on his Varsity. This made for balance and gave everyone a good workout. He had learned the system in the camps of the big league teams during a clinic he had attended in Arizona, and it seemed to be working well—possibly a little too well.

His Varsity hitters had not yet scored a run off the second-string pitching of Al Birkie, a tricky little south-paw. On the other hand, the Yannigans had managed two runs off right-handed Tod Hunter, a stout boy who needed to lose a few pounds before getting into shape.

Now, in this situation, in the fifth inning of what Coach Johnson intended to be a seven-inning workout, he wanted to see his strong boys get the lead, prove them-selves equal to facing Valley Conference rivals, then go on to the city playoffs. He scowled, calling to Harry Keel, "Hit away, Harry. Make it good, boy."

He was well aware that, with one out and a man on and a good hitter coming up, the percentage called for the bunt. But he was impatient with the inability of his chosen first-teamers to score. He scowled down at the shortstop-second base combination which had helped to stop them.

The shortstop, fitted in a last year's uniform which was a size too large, was a new kid, a transfer, a seventeen-year-old junior. He had olive skin, brown eyes, jet-black hair and very white, even teeth. He was narrow of shoulder but very long in the arms. His name was Jose Cansino.

The second-sacker was even slimmer, and he was also much shorter in stature. His skin was parchment color. His eyes were slanted. He was neatly put together, in perfect proportion, like a doll. He was only sixteen, and his arms and legs and wrists and hands seemed frail. His name was Aki Matsuo.

On the mound, Al Birkie squeezed the ball. He looked behind him at the infielders, the outfielders. He checked the runner on first. He was exceedingly cool and collected. He, too, was a senior. He was a veteran of the race last year, when Studio City had been nosed out in the local league.

Harry Keel grinned and confidently waggled his bat. The fielders settled themselves, taut and ready. Fred Barker, the sturdy, compact catcher, gave his sign. Birkie nodded and toed the slab.

At the fence, Junior, the Saint Bernard, made a decision. No one was coming to let him in. No one was paying any attention to him. After a few tentative yaps, he opened his mouth and really barked. Still no one seemed to care.

He had gone to a lot of trouble to get here and had used about the limit of the patience at his disposal. Like all of his breed, he was a gentle and tolerant dog, but enough was enough.

In fact, it was too much. He backed off five or six

lengths and cocked his eye at the gate. He bent his head, lowered one shoulder and advanced.

At first he seemed to be merely lumbering. Then he picked up speed. When he hit the gate, he was going at a rate which would have surprised anyone who happened to be watching.

The slim chain snapped. The gate flew wide.

Junior went with speed unimpeded toward the playing field. He passed the right fielder in a large blur of motion, throwing up dust beneath his enormous pads. He headed straight for the person he had come all this distance, through so much hindrance, just to see and comfort.

At that moment, Birkie pitched.

Harry Keel slammed through on the ball. He topped it just a bit. It was going down to shortstop. It was a perfect double-play ball. Jose Cansino had been eating up this kind of bounce ever since they had given him the slightly used, oversized uniform. Aki Matsuo was making for second to take the toss and snap his own throw to complete the play which would retire the varsity and leave them still scoreless.

It was then that Junior came off the grass and onto the skinned infield. He saw the ball. He chortled in his shaggy throat. He leaped and grabbed, his jaws yawning like an alligator.

The ball vanished. A wild yell went up. Junior spun, delighted at the applause. He ran past third base, recovered his balance and whirled around. He raced back and jumped up on his confidant, friend and brother.

Jose Cansino, stunned already by the unexpected intrusion, went down flat on his back under the fond attack. Junior dropped the wet ball and licked the cheek of his master.

Aki Matsuo picked up the ball. Jack Pilgrim, grinning from ear to ear, was on second. Harry Keel, doubled up with laughter, was on first. The Coach was coming onto the field, storming.

"Whose mutt is that?" demanded Chuck Johnson.

Jose struggled from under Junior and got to his feet. He was thoroughly angry. He snapped, 'That is no mutt, Señor Johnson. That is a fine dog named Junior."

Johnson swallowed. "Your dog?"

"Indeed, he is my dog." Jose was having trouble keeping the oversize shirt on straight. It had become unbuttoned and had slipped around his body. He tugged at it, his temper rising. "He has a pedigree. His father was a champion."

Junior wagged his tail.

Coach Johnson said frigidly, "I'm sure he's a fine dog. But he should not be allowed on the streets without a leash. That's the law."

Jack Pilgrim called over, "Hey, Coach, leave him alone. He's on *our* side. He broke up the double play!"

Now Chuck Johnson could not refrain from smiling. When he did so, the entire ball squad broke into laughter. There was some applause. Jose Cansino turned upon them angrily. His eyes flashed like beacons. He jammed the tail of his shirt into the pants which were threatening to leave their moorings. He shoved his worn fielder's glove into the capacious rear pocket. He took Junior by the collar and led him firmly off the diamond.

He did not stop there. He continued directly to the fence. He removed his spiked shoes. Then, still holding onto the dog, in his stocking feet, he set out toward his home, a mile away.

Someone yelled, "Sorehead!"

Coach Johnson roared, "That's enough of that. Let's get back to the ball game."

Aki Matsuo asked politely, "Is everybody safe, then?"

For some reason, that set everyone off to laughing again. Aki looked at them reproachfully. His English was perfect. He had been brought up in the United States, but sometimes his reactions were quite Oriental.

Coach Johnson answered, "No. Jack, go back to first. Harry, you go to the plate again. We'll take it from there —no strikes, no balls, one out." He looked around, then beckoned to a young boy on the bench. "Jay Byron, you play short."

The boy started, flushed, then ran out on the field. His glove was painfully new, despite repeated rubbings with oil. His spikes shone. He was a member of the tenth grade who had starred in Little League ball as a second baseman. He was no shortstop.

Harry Keel proved this a moment later when he knocked a grass-cutter directly between poor Jay Byron's legs and drove Harry Keel to third.

Joe Sampson then hit a home run.

It was Jack Pilgrim, however, who walked halfway out to the fence when the long inning was over and the

Varsity had scored five runs. He looked down the street, shook his head, then took his position in center field.

The little Mexican-American, he thought, had a lot on the ball. He stood up to people. He had been born down below the Border and he had kinda funny ideas about some things. Like he didn't hold still for jokes. Maybe he didn't understand jokes, the kind that were a big deal in Studio City High. But he was proud and he was a better fielder than Syd Grimm, the Varsity shortfielder.

In fact, Jack Pilgrim felt sympathetic toward Jose Cansino. He didn't know why, but there it was. If the kid could hit a little, he'd be a real great ballplayer—but that wasn't all of it.

And that dog of his, that Junior, he was a gasser. Stealing the ball like that. If he could have thrown to Aki, the double play would have been completed.

Jack Pilgrim found himself laughing softly. But he was not laughing *at* Jose and his Saint Bernard, he was laughing *with* them.

2

Since Studio City was the first town off the Freeway
going west from Los Angeles, and since the population
had increased by leaps and bounds during the past few
years, the high school was brand-new. It was a four-year
school, combining the ninth through the twelfth grades,
after which, presumably, graduates were ready for college.

The building itself was three stories high and of Spanish architecture. It was yellow stucco, with huge windows
dormered cunningly so that they might not seem stark
and cold. The grounds were huge, like most things in
Southern California, including a stadium for sports which
seated ten thousand people. Most students considered
themselves lucky to be part of this institution of learning.

Jack Pilgrim was one of these. The big, light-haired
center fielder and Student Body president arrived early

each morning on his bicycle. He was the proud possessor of an automobile, but he preferred the bike because it kept his legs and lungs in condition.

One morning, he rode into the yard, found his parking spot in the long rack, attached a padlock to his British racing model and looked around. No other student was in sight.

Lion, however, came running, growling, mewing. It was hard to tell whether or not the cat was pleased. He was not a creature who catered to people. He was bat-eared and slightly bowed in the front legs, and he weighed eighteen sturdy pounds. He had whiskers like a pirate and one of his eyes was badly squinted—the result of a fight with a bull terrier.

Lion was the campus cat. He had come with the building. The construction gang had fed him and he had just stayed on. He was not quite a mascot. He had too much dignity for such nonsense. He did not make friends, he merely suffered acquaintances. He kept other cats, stray dogs and hungry crows from the foliage which was burgeoning under the soft California sunshine.

Jack Pilgrim reached into the sack which he carried behind the seat of his bike and produced an oily paper bag. Lion settled down to a small roaring purr. There was a metal dish concealed behind the bicycle rack. Jack emptied the remains of last night's dinner at the Pilgrim home into the platter. Without the slightest recognition of his benefactor, Lion crouched, extended his bull-like neck and began to eat, with surprising daintiness for such a formidable creature.

Jack said, "Probably caught a field mouse last night, huh? Or maybe a rabbit? Or did you eat a small dog?"

Lion's deep, guttural sound seemed to say, "Can't you let a guy alone when he's eating?"

Jack continued, "I can't make up my mind about you, Lion. Either you're the world's least satisfactory cat or you're a champion."

It made him feel good to feed Lion each morning. He even carried a can opener, in case there were no leftovers, so that he might stop and buy a tin of cat food for his ungrateful friend. He watched awhile, enjoying the clear air of the morning.

The first of his teammates to arrive was Syd Grimm, who drove an old woody, a rebuilt station wagon which they often used for surfing. Jack watched as Syd parked the car and walked from the lot to where he waited. The Varsity shortstop was a square-built, husky figure, slightly bowed in the legs, heavy through the torso. His nose was rather flat and his dark eyes were set wide apart, giving him an owlish aspect.

"Hi, Jack!"

"Fine, Syd. What you know?"

"I don't know nothin'." This year, it was considered very clever in some circles to use double negatives. "Except we've got a good team going for us."

"Pretty good." Jack nodded.

"You wouldn't say real good?"

"Not without some better fielding," Jack answered bluntly.

Syd frowned. "I can't help it if Abe Cohen is slow on the pivot." Abe was the second baseman.

"Oh, it'll work out," Jack assured him. "Only, you both ought to practice more."

"I got things to do, man. I can't spend all my extra time teachin' Abe how to get the throw away."

Jack glanced at the old wooden station wagon in the parking space. "Sure. Whatever you say. I'm not the boss around here."

Syd shuffled his feet. "Sometimes you bother me, Jack. Sometimes it's like you're the teacher, or something."

"Not me. I mind my own business. You brought it up about the team, how good it is."

"Well, it's good enough. We'll win the title this year, you see if we don't." Syd rolled off toward the entrance to the school, walking a bit pigeon-toed. He was not the best runner on the team, nor the best hitter, either. But he was a veteran from last year and he knew the game. He was cool and never threw the ball around, like all the green kids would do.

Aki Matsuo was next to arrive, walking in his precise manner, books under his arm, looking straight ahead, inscrutable. He said, "Good morning, Jack."

"Hi, Aki. Got your homework?"

"As always." Aki seldom smiled. "And you, too. It is well known, those who prepare do not worry about eligibility."

"You're so right. Tell me, did you see Jose last night?" asked Jack.

"No, he does not live near my house."

"Oh—I thought you and he were friends. You play so

well together, I thought maybe you worked out together."

"Oh, no," said Aki, in some surprise. "It is perhaps because we have some experience at our positions."

"I see." Jack thought for a moment while Aki waited politely. "Look, I hate to see the kid quit. I mean, it's not easy for him, being the only Mexican in the school."

Aki did not blink as he replied, "And because I am the only Japanese, you think I might go to him and console him?"

"I didn't mean that," said Jack, contrite. "I don't think he needs consolation. He's got a quick temper and maybe he doesn't understand as much as you do."

Aki relaxed, almost grinned. "Thank you, Jack. I have had advantages which do make it easier for me. But I am afraid I cannot help where Jose is concerned."

"Okay, forget it," said Jack. He made a gesture as Aki departed. He had been thinking about Jose Cansino ever since the affair of the Saint Bernard dog. He was worried, although he did not quite know why, any more than he knew what to do about it. He felt a strong responsibility toward the team and the school and the Coach because he had been elected head of the student organization and the baseball team. He scowled at Lion.

The big cat had finished eating and was licking his chops, then using one paw to cleanse himself. Lion was a very clean cat, tiger-striped, with a white belly. He did not bother to look at his benefactor.

"You just don't care," said Jack, a bit envious. "You grab everything in sight and think it's your just due. Sometimes I really do worry about you."

There were other students arriving now. Among them,

Jack caught sight of a forlorn figure. He recognized Jose Cansino. The second-string shortstop was carrying a package, neatly wrapped, and heading for the entrance to the gymnasium. There was still a half hour before the first bell. Jack hurried in pursuit.

Coach Johnson's office was in a corner of the gym area, next to the dressing room. When Jack made his way through the tiers of metal lockers, he was just in time to see Jose tap on the door. He immediately ran to join him.

"Good morning, Jack," said Jose, low-voiced.

"Hi, kid! You going to see the Coach?" It was a kind of stupid question, but the best Jack could manage because of his instant worriment.

The door opened before Jose could answer, and Chuck Johnson regarded them, expressionless. They entered the office. Jose put his package on the wide desk.

"Good morning, boys," Johnson said. "Jose, what's the bundle?"

"My uniform," answered Jose. He was blinking, as though near to tears, but he spoke firmly enough. "My mama washed it clean."

"Now, what would we want with your uniform?" Jack interposed. "You've got to be kidding."

Jose said, "I am not sorry about my dog. But I cannot excuse myself for running away. A good person does not run away. He stays and does his job."

Jack said, "Why, you had to take the dog home. Like Coach says, it's against the law for him to be running loose. What else could you do?"

"Someone could have held my dog. I could have finished the practice, no?" Every so often, Jose fell into the Latin habit of ending his sentences with "no" or "yes" in the form of a question. It annoyed him when he did so, because he wanted to be like the others, the Anglos, as his parents called them. He had been brought all the way across town, out into the Valley, to go to school with the Americanos, and he wanted to join them. It was not easy.

Jack, sensing all this, said quickly, "Look, Coach, we shouldn't have laughed. Jose, here, he's a sensitive guy."

"I am no different than you, or the others," Jose asserted.

"I didn't say that," Jack objected.

Then the Coach interposed. "Jose, there is no need for you to turn in your uniform. There was no harm done yesterday. I'm sure your dog will be restrained from now on."

"It is difficult for my mama to keep Junior restrained," Jose told him sadly. "He is very strong—very strong. He is also smart."

Jack could not help adding, "And a great infielder."

"For years I practiced—against a wall, in the fields. He has always chased the ball," Jose told them. "He is, as you say, very good at catching the ball."

Coach Johnson felt that the conversation was getting away from him. He cleared his throat to attract the boys' attention and went on, "You have a future here in baseball, Jose. If you can learn to hit, you are certain of being next year's shortstop."

Jack said, "Nobody wants you to quit."

Jose looked him in the eye. "Nobody?"

"Not anybody I know." Jack stirred uneasily.

There was a small pause. Then Jose said, "It is that Coach Johnson and you, Jack, the captain, do not wish me to leave?"

"That's right." Jack and the Coach spoke together.

Jose bowed with the grace of a matador. He picked up the uniform, turned to the door. "Then I thank you and I withdraw my resignation." He went into the locker room, leaving the Coach and the captain staring at one another.

After a moment, Johnson asked, "What did he mean about somebody not wanting him on the squad?"

Jack squirmed. "Well, you know some kids are—well, prejudiced."

"Yes, but I don't like it."

"Neither do I. Both Aki Matsuo and Jose have heard some cracks. It's hard for some people to adjust."

"And you don't mean Jose or Aki." Chuck Johnson looked fondly at his captain, realizing gratefully that this boy had quality. "I'll leave all that to you. I think you can handle it," he said.

"I wouldn't bet on that." Jack was uncomfortable. "Supposing it's some of the seniors? Guys we need? Supposing it could cost us the championship if we interfere?"

Chuck Johnson's jaw jutted. "You know the answer to that."

Jack nodded. "Thanks, Coach. That's the way I was brought up. My father fought in the big war. He says all men are equal, only some are more equal than others, because the others are bigoted."

"Your father is a man of good sense," agreed Johnson. "Now you'd better get going. The bell is about to ring."

He was right. Just then, the warning bell sounded. Jack made for his homeroom on the double.

The corridors were empty, since he was so late in reaching the third floor. As he headed for Room 312, hustling toward the turning which would lead him to his goal, he heard running feet around the corner. He decided that someone else was a bit late, too.

Then the fire alarm went off. Jack stopped short. It seemed an odd time to call a drill.

On the other hand, the building was comparatively new and the authorities were always trying to make things safe for the students and perhaps filing out in lines from the homerooms was a good experiment. He began to run, skidded making the corner. Then he stopped short once more.

There were, in this modern complex, fire alarms on every floor. They were housed in conventional red boxes, behind glass which must be broken in an emergency. Jack had halted in fragments of glass that were scattered over the floor, under the box.

He remembered the flying feet. He sniffed, trying to find out from which way the smoke was coming. Only pure, washed air from the conditioners met his nostrils. Then the home rooms were emptying themselves as the student body marched in orderly, military fashion to the fire exits.

Jack fell into his proper place with his roommates. His heart was pounding, however, as they went down the fireproof stairs to the campus and the open air. He saw frowns on the faces of Coach Johnson, the Principal and his assistants in the front office.

There was certainly no fire. Somebody had set a false alarm.

If he had been a moment earlier or a few steps quicker, Jack realized, he would have seen the culprit—or culprits. He could not be sure whether he had heard one set of flying feet or more. Since he was wearing moccasins with composition soles, his own progress had been silent, therefore not overheard by the guilty party or parties.

He could go to the authorities and tell what he had heard. Then there would be a check on each home room, to see who was last in reporting—and who did not report at all. On the other hand, supposing it was some outsider who had played the dangerous prank? Sometimes dropouts who had been unable to find jobs and who were truthfully lonely and restless, wishing they were back in school, would enter the grounds and hang around until asked to leave. If it was someone like that, Jack certainly did not want to create a fuss and possibly trouble for innocent fellow students.

He decided to keep his own counsel. There was small damage done and the teachers would be checking out, in any case.

Then it occurred to him, as though someone had slugged him, that he, Jack Pilgrim, would be the prime suspect!

He had been in the corridor when the alarm sounded. He had bits of glass in the soles of his shoes, probably, if anyone bothered to look.

When Jack followed the others back into the school building, a while later, he saw Mr. Avery, his homeroom teacher, staring at him and he realized the word was already out that someone had rung up a false alarm. He braced himself, knowing he must tell the truth.

Yet, he thought, he need not say anything about running feet. He had, after all, not seen anyone.

There was only one clue. He had the athlete's sense of rhythm and timing. He also had excellent hearing. He was certain that one of the runners had been a big fellow, and that he had flat feet. The slap-slap of shoes on the hard corridor floor had been unmistakable. People with high arches run on their toes. This person was running hard on his heels.

3

That afternoon, baseball practice began late, because the fire department people and the police had been asking questions all over the school. Coach Johnson was not in a good mood while he was separating his players into groups, trying to teach them basic baseball, trying to get them to loosen up their swings at bat, trying to get their full attention when he knew they were thinking about the false alarm.

He called out, "Jack, take the batting cage for me, will you? Let Birkie pitch and make 'em hit to the opposite field for a while."

The first-team infield was about to take practice, with Johnson hitting fungoes. Syd Grimm paused to speak to Jack. "I see the Mex sneaked back."

"Watch your language, man." Jack spoke sharply. "The kid's all right."

"You sure are a bossman," Syd said, shaking his head.

"You sure look after them all, don't you? A real baby sitter. The Jap and the Mex and everybody."

Jack asked, "Are you looking for trouble with me?"

For a second, the dark, squat boy seemed ready to accept the challenge. Then he said, "Someday, man, someday I'll take you up on that. I hate a bossman."

Jack watched him slop onto the field, arrogant, too sure of himself. These two had known each other a long time, even before they had come to Studio City High. They had played and surfed together, double-dated, visited with each other. Jack wondered when Syd had started to dislike him. Was it when he had been elected captain?

Or was it when he began to take an interest in Jose Cansino?

While going to the batting cage, off to one side of the diamond, he thought it must be the latter. He could scarcely believe it, but Syd was intolerant of the boys from other racial backgrounds. This was utterly silly, but there was no getting around it, Jack knew.

Birkie was out on the mound of the practice field with a basketful of used balls. Jack looked around for a catcher. Little Jay Byron was lurking in the background, a rosy-cheeked sophomore. He came when Jack beckoned and agreed to don mask and protector. He looked tiny back of the plate, but Birkie couldn't fool him with easy curves, and he held onto the fast ball. A real prospect, Jack felt, a comer for the future teams at Studio City High.

Then he scowled. Maybe he was a sort of bossman in his mind. He thought about others, worried about them, speculated about times to come. Was that wrong?

He saw Jose Cansino and dismissed such troublesome thoughts. He said, "All right, Jose. You're the hitter."

Jose was nervous. He was carrying a twenty-eight-ounce bat with a lot of whip. He looked very slender, even skinny, standing at the plate. He did bat left-handed, which was a good sign, Jack knew.

Birkie, always working on his pitching assortment, threw a soft curve. Jose lunged at it, fouled it off.

Jack said, "Just throw some straight balls, Al. We're trying to hit to spots."

Birkie asked, "Over the center?"

"This is for the batters, not the pitchers," Jack reminded him.

"All right, bossman," said Birkie cheerfully.

Jack started, then realized that the left-handed pitcher, an easy-going boy, meant nothing by the remark.

Jose hit at a hard, fast one. He again fouled it back into the net. Jack knelt to watch the action of the thin kid's swing.

Birkie threw a slower pitch. Jose stepped into it and hit it to left field, which was the proper way to go with the pitch.

Jack said, "All right, next."

Joe Sampson, the big, hard-slugging left fielder, strode to the plate. He proceeded to hit the ball to right, to center, and to left, smartly bouncing grounders.

Jack had Jose by the elbow. "You see the way he levels on the line of the pitch? He's a natural, of course. But you can do it."

Jose, swinging the light bat, tried to emulate Sampson. Jack shook his head.

"Not quite, but you're getting it. Let me see that bat."

Someone yelled, "Hey, Jack, who's next?"

"Line up," he said. "What do you want, a nurse?"

The bat Jose had been wielding felt like a toothpick in his hands. He whipped it around. Then he had an idea.

He asked, "Do you always use this light stick? Let's try something."

He went to the bats laid out in a row on the ground and found one of his own specials. It weighed thirty-two ounces. There was not much whip in the handle, but it felt solid and right in his grip.

He said, "You've got long arms and big hands for a skinny kid. Want to take a chance?"

Jose gravely accepted the bat. He wrapped his pliant fingers around it. He experimented, swinging. His dark eyes brightened. Something inside him began to expand a little. He said, "I never tried. They always gave me light bats, because I am, as you say, skinny."

"Go behind the cage," Jack suggested. "Watch the pitches and take your cuts. Try it for a while and we'll get you back to take some real swings again."

"*Gracias, señor,*" Jose said. He could have bitten off his tongue then, because he was determined to forget the Spanish expressions and use English only. He was astounded when Jack grinned widely as he walked away. The big captain of the team seemed to enjoy being thanked in the soft Latin language.

Behind the cage, Jose could see the pitches plainly

enough to guess where they were going. He took his stance and began trying to level the bat through on the plane of each. It was absorbing work. He was perspiring and did not realize it. He was also enjoying the feel of the heavier stick. It seemed to have more authority, as if there were good, clean hits built into it.

Jack came back after a while and said, "Okay, everybody else has taken his cut. Let's try it."

Jose went to the plate. Birkie was working easily, and with fine control.

Jack said, "All right, low on the outside. Hit it to left, Jose."

Birkie delivered. Jose followed the course of the ball, swung mightily. He missed.

Jack came behind him and instructed, "You're slugging. Just meet the ball. Same pitch, Al."

Birkie obliged. Jose saw every stitch on this one. He came around carefully, met the ball. It went into right field, sharp and clean.

"Try it again."

It was as if someone had opened a box and inside there was a stack of gaudy goodies, Jose thought. Again and again he hit the ball. The bigger bat did not require as much whip and stress. The ball met the good wood and went merrily off to spots where it would count for a hit. It got better and better, until Jose suddenly came awake and saw Coach Johnson was watching, as were the members of the Varsity infield. He fell back in confusion, thinking he had upset the entire practice.

But Johnson only said, "Okay, second string take the

field. Varsity infield take batting practice. Get another pitcher. Birkie, cover up your arm."

Jack walked to the diamond with Jose. "How'd it feel?"

"It is like day and night," Jose answered wonderingly. "It is like sunrise and sunset. It is like sunshine and rain. It is magnificent."

"If it works, it's magnificent, all right," Jack told him. "I'm going to hit some fungoes to you now. Work on that double play with Aki, huh? Can't ever get it down too good, you know."

"True," said Jose. "So true . . . and thank you again."

"It's okay, *amigo.*" Jack grinned.

Then as he turned to pick up the loaded fungo bat, he was aware that Syd Grimm was watching him with a dour, contemptuous expression. Joe Sampson was standing beside the first-string shortstop, and the two exchanged muttered words, then a mocking laugh. Jack glared at them until they sobered and walked away.

He knew they were criticizing his attentions to Jose. He tried to see their point of view. Since they wouldn't be back next year, they probably thought it was silly to bother with the younger fellows. They were . . . selfish? Thoughtless? Uncaring? Was that the way people were supposed to be nowadays?

A thought suddenly struck him between the eyes, blurring the field, the ball, everything. Syd Grimm was flat-footed. Whoever had pulled the false alarm ran on the flat of his feet.

He shook off the thought. Syd was acting in a most peculiar manner, but he was not the kind of delinquent who would set off a false alarm.

Or was he?

Jack seemed to be asking himself a lot of serious questions these days. He picked up the thin bat and began knocking grounders to the infield. In a moment, he was absorbed in the job, forgetting all else.

He knocked a dozen balls down to Jose, who relayed them to Aki Matsuo with an underhand whip. In turn, Aki touched the bag, wheeled and whipped a throw to first base. The two worked like a team of acrobats. With a little more seasoning, they would be ready for Varsity play. None of the other candidates seemed to have much class, Jack thought, but little, willing Jay Bryon and this pair would surely make it after he had gone on to college.

The Coach's whistle sounded a loud blast. Everyone quit what he was doing and started around the field on a trot. It was a huge enclosure, and after a workout it seemed miles, but no one dreamed of shirking the routine. This was good for the legs and Johnson had pounded the idea into the athletes early in his association with them.

Jack Pilgrim ran with the others. Ahead of him were Syd Grimm and Joe Sampson, side by side. He noticed with growing alarm that Joe was also a heel-and-toe man, with fallen arches.

This, he decided, was nonsense. A lot of boys who frequented the beaches, walking barefoot in the sand, developed flat feet. He put the thought away in the far reaches of his mind and doggedly ran out the required distance, with a sprint at the end.

Jose Cansino and Aki led all the others in this part of the day's workout. They finished neck and neck at the

door of the gym, yards in the lead. It was another indication that they had a future in Studio City High School
athletics.

In the dressing room, Coach Johnson again blew for
attention and, at the shrill sound, everyone paused and
listened. He said, "I want you all to hear this. The incident today in the school was a disgrace." He paused, then
went on, "I am not for a moment suggesting that any of
you had any knowledge of it. I would be shocked and
astounded if you did. Athletes don't lower themselves in
that manner. But I do want you to know that a trick like
that costs the taxpayers, your fathers and mothers, many
hundreds of dollars. The fire department, the police department have to attend to it, and whatever they do is
costly. So, if you do find out anything about this needless,
criminal prank—come to me and tell me about it."

No one spoke. Jack felt a guilty pang, but decided that
he would keep silence because, actually, he knew nothing
conclusive.

The Coach continued, "Now, we all know that next
week we open the season against Bellingham High. We
realize how important this is, that Bellingham has one of
the best teams in the Valley. We want to get off to a good
start. We'll play one game at a time, but we want that
championship, all of us. We think we have a chance to get
it. We're experienced as a club. We don't throw the ball
around wildly. We know how to play the game. If we lose
this one, we're in trouble. We're the favorites—and
rightly so. This week's workouts can tell the story. I want
every man on his toes every minute of the time. I want

every little detail checked out, down to your spikes. Everything must fit, everything must be perfect. We'll leave nothing to chance. Their pitcher, Jossman, is great. I'm not sure yet whether we'll use Tod Hunter against him or start with Birkie and bring in a right-hander later on. I'm going to watch you all during the workouts and make up my mind. The first team is pretty well set—but changes can be made. I promise you, anyone goofing off for one minute will sit on the bench. If we're not serious about the championship, there's no use taking the field. Is that clear?"

The boys all nodded. A couple shouted, "We're with you, Coach."

Chuck Johnson concluded, "All right, get your showers, then go home and do your allotted book work. I want you all to be eligible, also. Work, work, work!"

He went into his office. There was silence for a moment, then Syd Grimm laughed, but not loud enough for the Coach to hear.

"Work, work, work!" he chanted. "Boy, I thought we were supposed to have fun." He bowed low to Jack, adding, "Now, don't you go and snitch, bossman."

Jack was down to his underwear. He went across the locker room and stood facing Syd. "You've been doing a lot of shooting off your mouth today, boy. I don't know what's eating you, but I have a big, fat message for you: Knock it off."

Syd shrugged, "You're mighty sensitive these days. Looks like you've got something bothering *you*."

"Maybe a lot of things are bothering me, but I don't need any big talk from you."

"Maybe you'd like me to quit the team," retorted Syd, flaring up as though a fuse had been lit. "Maybe you'd like your greaser friend to play shortstop."

Jack picked him up then. He grabbed him by the T-shirt and pushed him against a locker. When Syd tried to hit back, Jack slapped him with his open hand. The sound could be heard all over the room. The Coach's door flew open.

Jack shouted, "Don't you call anyone a name like that. Don't you dare! I'll beat your brains out if you ever do that again!"

Johnson ordered, "Grimm! Pilgrim! In here, this minute."

There wasn't another sound in the room as the two boys marched into the Coach's sanctum. They stood on opposite sides of the room, Syd with his face flaming from the cuff dealt him, Jack still seething with anger.

The door reopened behind them. Jose Cansino came into the office. The trio stared at him.

Jose said, "Please, this is not right. If Syd wishes to call me 'greaser,' then it is between him and me, is it not?"

Coach Johnson said carefully, "No one is allowed to use such expressions on my teams!" He turned to Syd. "Is that clear?"

The squat shortstop answered, "That's none of your business. That's my business. Maybe even it's Jack's business, if he wants to make something out of it. But it's none of your business. You're the Coach, that's all."

Johnson sighed. "You believe that, do you? I'm just here to put a baseball team together?"

"That's it," said Grimm. "You're a coach. You teach baseball. That's it."

Johnson thought for a long moment. He could see his championship drifting away. He could see the end of his present dream to be noticed, maybe promoted to a college job. He did not falter, however. "All right, Syd. Turn in your uniform."

The shortfielder shook his head. "I don't have to. My father's a taxpayer. He'll have something to say about this —to the Board of Education."

"Yes, I'm sure he will," said Johnson wearily. "Ideas like yours have to begin in the home." He turned to the other two. "All right, you're excused. Jose, you'll work out with the Varsity from now on. That's all."

He went back to the papers on his desk. The three boys filed out, sober, their thoughts turned inward, not looking at each other. It was a bad ending for the day.

• • • • • 4 • • • • • • • • • • • • • • • •

Jose Cansino's father, who was a successful lawyer, had chosen thoughtfully and well in buying his home in Studio City. Junior, the Saint Bernard, was aware of this, at least he knew it was a better place than the one he had lived in before. The house was on a corner and there was a large yard. The only trouble was, around the yard ran a high fence.

The other problem was the gate. Unlike the wire gate at the school, where he had enjoyed such great success, this one was barred with a large steel bolt. No matter how often he tried, he could not get out of that yard.

His only chance, he realized, was that one of the two other children of Papa and Mama Cansino, who were much younger than Jose, would forget and leave the bolt out of its socket. This had happened on that other fine occasion. There had been a small fuss about it, but the Cansinos were kindly people, full of love for children and animals, and it was soon over.

What they did not understand was how much his young master needed the devoted dog. They did not know about the long "talks," one of which was now taking place—about the exchange of sentiments between Junior and Jose. In fact, Jose himself seemed somewhat uncomprehending these days, at least he never took Junior to that fascinating play place with him, not even once, not even for a little while.

It was very disappointing for Junior to find this flaw, this lack of sympathy, in one who was so close to him, but Junior was a true Cansino, loving and forgiving.

Jose was saying, "The Coach is liable to get into trouble. Jack Pilgrim has been up before Mr. Vale, the principal. And to make it worse, Abe Cohen and I do not make the double play as well as Aki and myself. It is a difficult situation."

Junior whimpered acknowledgment that he understood. Jose was not happy.

"Abe is a very nice fellow," Jose went on earnestly. "It is just that we have not had practice together. Abe can hit the ball very well, much better than Aki or myself. It is up to me, that is the problem. I must make myself fit into the team. It is not for the team to fit into me." He added mournfully, "And I am not a great hitter. Better, yes, good —no. Everyone is very nice to me, you must understand. It is all my problem."

Junior yawned. It was early in the morning and he had spent a long night walking around the yard, chasing cats. There were too many cats in the world. He did not care for cats. He had never really known one and he was not sure as to what he would do if he should happen to catch one, but he knew they were inimical to him.

Jose patted his head and said, "I must go now. You be good and mind what Mama tells you and I will see you this evening."

The trouble was, Junior thought, that the days seemed too long. It was lonely in the back yard. The younger children, Maria and Miguel, were all right, but they were not like Jose. Their games grew tiresome after a while and they were not mature enough to be good, solid company for a growing young Saint Bernard. They talked to each other and they talked *at* him. They were not old enough to talk *to* him.

Jose went absently to the gate, and Junior's left ear flopped up as he watched. The bolt could not be managed from outside. Jose made sure it was fastened and then said, "Now, behave yourself, Junior."

The boy went through the house on his way to school and the dog sat down and scratched his right ear with his right hind leg, not an easy job for an animal with his build. He fell over after a moment and just lay there, stretched out like a rug, dissatisfied with recent events.

At the school, Jack Pilgrim fed shredded fish to the cat named Lion, saying, "It's Friday and you eat fish because it's all I could get for you. I know you'd rather have liver, but not today."

It was true that Lion really did not care much for fish. He had peculiar eating habits. He rumbled a bit in his throat and pecked at the food on his plate. Jack watched him for a while, until he saw Jose coming and called to him. Jose, had been running fifty paces, then walking fifty, as indicated in the *Boy Scout Manual,* while covering the mile between his home and the playground, so he was slightly out of breath.

Jack said, "More bad news."

"You're not in trouble because of me?" Jose's expression was pleading.

"Oh, that. Nothing, man, nothing at all. Syd's father and all his uncles couldn't get anywhere. The Coach knocked them out of the box. Syd's off the team, that's it."

"Then what is the trouble?"

Jack answered, "Abe Cohen's family is moving. His father works for Consolidated Aviation, you know. They're going to Northern California right now, government contract. It happens all the time in that business."

"But we need Abe."

"Yeah. Aki's all right, but he can't hit. I guess you'll be glad to work with him again."

"Yes, I can play well with him." Just the same, Jose was disconsolate. "It is ironic. We should be very happy to be on the Varsity. But if we cannot hit, we will be very unhappy because we are bad for the team."

Jack thought about this for a moment, then shook his head. "The team is lucky to have two good fielders to fill in. Look at it that way."

"Thank you. But it is not enough."

"We'll have a long batting practice this afternoon. Tomorrow—well, we'll just have to see what happens. Bellingham's got great pitching."

Jose said, "It makes me nervous to think about it."

"Sure, nervous. You're not scared?"

Jose looked surprised. "But nobody should play the game if he is scared, no, Captain Jack?"

"My sentiments, exactly, man."

They smiled at one another. At this moment, Syd Grimm and Joe Sampson came by, paused and stared rudely at the pair. Jack took a step forward and stared right back. Lion came from behind the rack, licking his chops.

Syd Grimm said, "Man, you're really nowhere now. You gone and lost your ball club."

"That's your opinion," replied Jack. "Wheel it away, will you?"

"I don't dig you at all," said Syd. "You've gone out of your silly mind, hanging around with these cats."

"Watch out!" Jack warned.

"Oh I got the message," replied Syd. "I know I can't say what I want to say." He laughed. "But you know what I mean, all right."

Jose now put down his books and moved forward. He said politely, "If you please, you will not trick Jack into a fight."

"I won't do what?" demanded Syd Grimm.

"It is an old trick," stated Jose firmly. "You think to aggravate Jack so that he will attack you. Then you will complain to the authorities."

"Well, what do you know? We've got a lawyer," said Syd Grimm.

"If you want to start a fight," Jose said distinctly, "you will direct your remarks at me."

The squat, heavily built boy stared. "You must be kidding, man."

"Believe me, I am quite serious."

"Why, I could eat you alive, squirt." Grimm made a threatening motion, then restrained himself. He cried, "Hey, I'm wise to you! I get it. You're trying to incite *me*. You want me to hit you, then you'll have a case to take to the Principal."

Jose allowed himself a flicker of a smile. "As you say, señor. As you say."

Joe Sampson guffawed. "Beat you to it that time, didn't he, Syd?"

Lion the cat walked with great, bowlegged grace between Jose and Syd, flaunting his fan of a tail. Jack Pilgrim said, "It's about time for the first bell. Come on. Syd's got a lot of thinking to do."

They started away. Joe Sampson fell in on the other side of Jose. Syd Grimm glared after them, then took a quick kick at the rear of Lion. The cat whirled about, hissing, and deftly tore a hole in Syd's trouser cuff with a sharp, curving claw, then he turned and vanished behind the bicycle rack, where he could get his back against the wall. Syd listened to the challenging growl of the big feline and decided he would ignore the entire affair.

At the entrance to the school, Joe Sampson said, "That was awful smart, Jose, puttin' Syd on the spot like that."

Jack told him, "Jose's father is a lawyer—a real good one. He's going to be a lawyer, too."

"What do you know about that?" marveled the big left fielder. "He sure put Syd down." Joe went off toward his home room.

Jack said, "Putting Syd down, that's nothing, *amigo.* Splitting Sampson away from him, that is something. There could have been more trouble if they kept hanging around together."

"Thank you, Captain Jack," said Jose. "I will not say it did not come to my mind."

Jack nodded. "Yes, I suppose it did. Come to think of it, I suppose it did occur to you." They winked at one another and went their respective ways.

The day was not any different from any other scholastic day—until almost the end. Then the fire alarm went off again.

This time, Jack Pilgrim was not as close to the box on the wall as before, but his reflexes sent him on a run in that direction. He skidded on the shattered glass, almost fell. He saw a piece of cloth on the floor. He picked it up as students and teachers came in droves.

Principal Vale restored order, and calls were made to police and fire departments. Mr. Vale was a tall, white-haired man of distinction, a veteran of the school system, not easily panicked. But when he called Jack into his office, he was thoroughly upset and made no bones about it.

"This is twice you've been the first one on the scene," he pointed out, "Have you any explanation?"

Coach Johnson was present, and Jack's home-room teacher, Mr. Avery, a young man of great seriousness. Both protested.

The Coach said, "It's not fair to attack Pilgrim."

Mr. Avery said, "I'm sure Jack had nothing to do with it."

The Principal glowered at them. "Gentlemen, I am not attacking Pilgrim, nor accusing him. I'm trying to get to the bottom of this serious business." He turned to Jack. "Well?"

For a long moment, Jack hesitated. Finally, he said, "The first time I did hear footsteps running away. This time—well, I just heard the bell, and I ran."

Mr. Vale asked, "Has it occurred to anyone that the culprit may be trying to lay the blame on Pilgrim?"

The others had not thought of that. They were stunned.

Mr. Vale continued, "This sort of act indicates an aberration. It may be that we have a student in this school who is mentally unbalanced. If so, it is for his own welfare that we must find him. It is not so much a matter of punishment as of correction. The results of this kind of act can be serious. Someone may well be hurt. There could be general fear and confusion. Think about it, gentlemen. The detective force of Los Angeles will be probing into it."

The three left, feeling a little as though they had been reprimanded and warned within an inch of their lives. Jack went to the locker room, hid himself behind his locker and took out the piece of cloth.

It looked like part of a pair of trousers. It was a small, three-cornered piece of beige material. Most of the boys wore to school pants made of this durable material which kept its crease even after laundering. It would be next to impossible to find the owner of the fragment.

Jack hesitated to turn it in. He was in dire fear of being a squealer or a busybody. He thought he might take a look around on his own, but something in him shrank from turning over a clue to the police. He could not bring himself to have any part in delivering up a fellow student —especially one who might be mentally ill, as Mr. Vale had said—to interrogation by detectives.

He had a feeling that he was wrong in his thinking. However, he put the swatch of cloth in his locker, underneath his spare outfielder's glove, and dressed for practice. He brooded over the matter all afternoon, which resulted in a letup in his hitting. His timing seemed to be off.

Coach Johnson was extremely unhappy with the workout. He told the team over and over that Bellingham High would beat them tomorrow if they did not snap out of it. He worked himself into a lather trying to get Aki Matsuo and Jose Cansino to meet the ball with a level swing, to follow the pitch, to try for singles, walks, anything to get on base.

Afterward, he went to his office to wrestle with a lineup which might have a chance against the visitors from deep in the Valley.

Saturday dawned bright and clear, with a few fleecy clouds high in the sky. Mama and Papa Cansino were up early, getting breakfast for the family, making preparations to have the afternoon free to see Jose play shortstop for the Varsity of the Studio City Green Sox against the Bellingham "Bells."

Junior was excited by this bustling atmosphere. It was necessary to talk to him and calm him down with the assurance that he would be allowed to attend the game if he would behave. He listened to Jose, but he could not quite contain himself. He jumped and frolicked with all the grace and agility of a performing elephant.

Jose said to him, "I almost wish you were not to be at the game. Nor my parents, nor my brother and sister. Supposing I were to fail? Supposing I lose the game for the team?"

Junior would not allow any such gloom to fall upon this

occasion, which he fully recognized as momentous and exciting. He licked Jose's cheek and danced away, lowering his head, inviting play.

Jose said, "At least you can believe in me." It made him feel better, but not completely confident.

Jack Pilgrim came by early. He was driving his car today, a seven-year-old Chevy which he had remodeled, a shining coupe, his pride and joy. He was extremely polite to Mama and Papa, who beamed upon him with approval as Maria and Miguel looked on, wide-eyed, in awe of the captain of the team. Jose drove off with him to the school grounds and the ball field.

Junior almost turned himself inside out at this faithless desertion. It took the entire family to calm him.

At the school grounds, Jack reached into the back of his car and brought out a package. For the first time that day, Jose smiled.

"You always think of Lion, the cat," he said.

"He's my pal," Jack told him. "What about your dog? Don't you feel that way about him?"

"Junior?" Jose frowned. "He is very close to me, but lately I do not see enough of him, because of baseball."

The two walked to the bicycle rack. Lion was waiting, pretending to ignore them in his lordly manner, but smacking his chops nevertheless. Jack emptied some assorted food on the metal plate. Lion aproached it with assumed disdain, then fell to with vigor.

Jack said, "No small prey last night, Lion? Or are you stoking up against the day? Worried I won't make it tomorrow?"

"Do you feed him on Sunday, also?"

Jack looked slightly embarrassed. "I usually manage to drive by and hand him something over the fence. The grounds are locked on Sundays, you know."

Jose said, "He is indeed your *amigo*. It is very thoughtful of you to do this." He regarded the cat with closer attention. "Lion is not very friendly to others, is he?"

"He's just independent." Jack was quick to defend his furry friend. "He's a kind of a loner, I guess. Maybe people don't understand him."

"A loner." Jose thought about this. "With one friend. *Sí*, this I can understand."

"Now, wait a minute! You're not like Lion."

"Am I not?"

Jack answered earnestly, "Well, there's a difference. You keep so busy all the time, and you are new here. The kids haven't had a chance to know you."

Jose was silent. Jack bit his lip. The similarity between the proud cat and the proud Latin was not far-fetched, at that.

Jack said, "Let's go and see if Coach is here."

Chuck Johnson had been there for some time. He looked up at them when they entered. He had a clean score sheet in his hand. He extended it to Jack without words.

It read:

CANSINO S.S.

HATFIELD R.F.

SAMPSON L.F.

PILGRIM	C.F.
KEEL	1st B.
FARMER	3rd B.
BARKER	C.
MATSUO	2nd B.
BIRKIE	P.

Looking over Jack's shoulder, Jose inhaled sharply. He was to lead off the season at bat for the Green Sox.

Johnson said, "It's this way: I want our heavy hitters up in a row. If they connect, we can break open the ball game in the first inning—or any other inning in which they come up in order. If Jose, who is light, can get on—and I figure he has a better chance than Matsuo or Birkie or the others—we can get off to a flying start."

"I see what you mean, Coach," said Jack. He looked dubiously at Jose. "You dig, *amigo?*"

"Maybe I will get hit in the head," said Jose solemnly. "Then we will have a big start, no?"

Coach Johnson grinned. It made him look younger and less grimly concerned. "With that attitude, we've got a chance. This Jossman, now, he's a fine pitcher. Just keep after him. Make him throw to you."

He broke off, shaking his head. Jack laughed a little. He had faced Jossman the year before. Jose waited, silent, for the others to say more.

Johnson merely told them, "Get dressed. It's only a ball game. I shouldn't pressure you. I've told you all this before."

"The Bells will be the team to beat," Jack said. "We know it's important, Coach."

"That's all I ask."

Coach Harry Aiken of Bellingham High came in then, a smiling, husky man, who had been at school with Chuck Johnson and once had a tryout with the Dodgers. The two shook hands, exchanging hearty insults as the two boys escaped to the locker room.

Jack went to the bulletin board and posted the line-up. Genial Al Birkie came in, slim, dark, confident, and began to read it with care. Fred Barker, his battery mate, joined him. Joe Sampson and graceful, tall Chris Hatfield, the transplanted Southerner who played right field, crowded around them.

Harry Keel came in, working at his first-baseman's fishnet glove, and then Nick Farmer, the third-sacker, entered, with Jay Byron following a discreet three steps behind him and blushing furiously at his temerity in even reading the names of those who would start today.

Aki Matsuo slipped in, making no noise as usual, and several of the second string came after him. There was not much confusion. Everyone was subdued before this first game, probably because it was against such a strong rival for the Valley title.

Tod Hunter, the right-handed pitcher, asked Jack Pilgrim, "What do you think?"

"About the line-up? Or about starting Birkie?"

"They've got a lot of hefty swingers," acknowledged Tod. "I guess Coach is right. He's going by the book."

"He'll have you in there if Birkie weakens, don't you worry about that."

"Oh, that's all right."

But Tod would have liked to start the season in the box,

Jack knew. Everyone's family would be here for the opener and, of course, each player wanted to show his ability. That was normal and human.

Sampson came by and asked, "You think Cansino should lead off? I mean, why not go right at 'em with the best?"

"I like it the way it is," Jack told him.

"It's only that the kid hasn't played in this league before."

"He played over in L.A., where the pitching is very good," Jack reminded him.

Sampson nodded and moved away, satisfied. Jose, partially hidden by his locker door, had overheard. He did not change expression. He finished dressing and sat in a corner, awaiting the Coach's orders. Jack adjusted his pants, folding them in the way he had been taught years ago in the Little League, down on his legs, but not ankle-length, as some players did. The strain was beginning to tell. He had not realized that, as captain, he would be asked so many questions. It was an added burden on such a day as this.

Coach Johnson came out, finally, and said very little to the team. "We want this one. Let's go out and warm up like pros. Show them we're ready. Everybody run now. Out you go!"

They ran out. The stands were filling up. Baseball is a big sport in Southern California, from Little League through college. Since the advent of both major leagues in the area, everybody was a partisan scout for one or the other of the teams. Everyone was also critical, even of high-school players.

The Green Sox took the field and began pregame warmup. The Bells were filing out and someone brought the line-up. The umpires were lounging in their car, transportation furnished by the city, if required. There was an air of brisk efficiency about the entire proceedings.

Jack led the team to the home bench and the visitors took the field. They were an agile and expert aggregation, as he knew from the previous year. He received a copy of their line-up from Coach Johnson and scanned it. It read:

KELLER	C.F.
OBER	R.F.
CARNEY	L.F.
SYKES	1st B.
ANTHONY	3rd B.
TOLER	S.S.
EBERLY	2nd B.
EINSTEIN	C.
JOSSMAN	P.

He realized that Coach Aiken was going right after the runs. The first four batters had proven themselves among the best in the league. Anthony, the third baseman, was a .265 hitter who could murder you in a clutch. Toler and Eberly were average. Then there was the catcher, Einstein, another who hit for .300 year in and year out.

As for Ed Jossman, he was a tall, rangy right-hander who had attracted big league scouts on his trail each season since he had pitched two no-hitters in the Babe Ruth League. He had a great fast ball and a curve which fell off the table. If he had a fault, it lay in his control, which went astray every so often—the same fault a lefty named Sandy Koufax had suffered under in his time.

This was the team the Green Sox were going up against with a rookie keystone combination which had never faced real competition. No wonder Coach Johnson looked so grave and concerned.

He took his own line-up out to the plate as the umpires appeared. The Bells had finished their workout and were assembled about Coach Aiken, getting a pep talk, Chuck Johnson supposed. After a moment, Jossman broke away and came to where the umpires and Jack Pilgrim waited. He was a husky, tall boy with rather heavy features and wide-spaced eyes which could narrow to slits when he was under pressure.

Jack said, "Hi, Ed!"

"Hi, Pilgrim!" Jossman was formal, ever the enemy. He did not believe in fraternizing.

"How's the arm?" Jack went on genially.

"Good enough." Jossman made it sound menacing.

The umpires filed the line-ups in their breast pockets, and Jossman retreated to the bench to cover himself with a windbreaker of silver and blue, the colors of Bellingham. Jack went to where his team was poised, taking off his jacket of green and white, the Green Sox hues. Al Birkie ground a ball in his slender hands.

Jose Cansino looked at the stands and found his family in the front row. Crouched before them, firmly leashed was Junior, his head up, eyes bright. Jose waved in a covert manner so as not to draw attention from the overflowing crowd.

Bellingham rooters had come from up the Valley and were assembled behind the visitors' dugout, making noise enough to send Lion, the cat, into retreat behind the bike rack. Coach Johnson barked a command and his team broke for the field in their natty, new white uniforms with green trim, green caps sporting a white SC, clean white sweat socks and new spikes. Jose had drawn his Varsity spangles only yesterday and for a moment was conscious of himself—the figure he was cutting at shortstop, the responsibility upon him to make good. Then Harry Keel bounced a warmup ball his way as Birkie took his pitches and he got the feel of the horsehide, the feel of firm dirt beneath his spikes, the warm feel of the sun, the deep, exultant feel of the game in which he was involved.

The head umpire called, "Play ball," and the spectators on both sides were cheering. Under it all, Jose could hear the throaty bark of Junior, a heartening sound. Birkie tugged at his cap, toed the rubber and faced Keller, the outfielder and leadoff man, a short, sturdy youth with limber wrists.

Birkie had a nice, easy motion for a slight left-hander, and his fast ball sneaked a little. He threw in close to the right handed batter. Keller swung and the ball came down to short, took a vicious hop and nearly went over Jose's shoulder.

He made his adjustment and grabbed the hot shot. It nearly turned him around. He had no play and he knew it.

He held onto the ball as the speedy Keller crossed first base, then walked over to Birkie and said, "I am sorry."

Birkie said coolly, "It was a hit, *amigo*. Good thing you didn't throw it—it might have got away."

A warm glow ran through Jose's blood stream at this reassurance. He returned to his position. Ober, another right-handed hitter, was at bat. Birkie checked, lifted his shoulders and threw a breaking ball.

The Bells had orders to slam at the first pitch. They were out to crush Birkie in the opening inning and set up a commanding lead. Jose understood this as Ober slammed through the curve ball. Again it came down to short, a little to the right, as though they were deliberately trying out the rookie.

Jose pounced, blocking the bounce. He wheeled and, with swift dexterity, underhanded the ball to Aki Matsuo.

Aki, already on the move, barehanded the easy toss and wheeled. As he did so, Keller barreled into him. Aki had to hurry his throw. Ober was safe. Aki arose and calmly dusted himself.

It was a legitimate block, both Jose and Aki knew, to break up the double play. Each settled back, shifting slightly for Carney, the Bells left fielder, a port side hitter. Birkie glanced at them, nodded at the runner, then settled in. He threw a hard, fast one, in around the wrists.

Carney slammed at it. He got a piece and the bouncer was to Aki, deep in the hole. Jose came to second and took the throw, a little high to his right, as Ober tried to take him out of the play. He leaped and threw for first in one motion. He fell across Ober as the Bells right fielder slid, dirtying his nice new uniform, then scrambled up, watching the umpire on the base line. He saw the thumb of the man in dark blue jerk over his shoulder and knew he had completed the first double play of the Green Sox season. His heart swelled with pride and joy. He ran off the field with the rest of the team, hearing the cheers and Jack Pilgrim yelling encouragement.

It was the first time Jose had ever really believed that he was on the team. It had all seemed chancy, sort of lucky, up until now. He had been under sufferance because of what had happened to Syd Grimm.

As he went to the bat rack to find the stick Jack had obtained for him, the heavy one, Jose saw Syd behind the wire of the grandstand. He noticed that there were three other boys with the former ballplayer and recognized them as dropouts, hangers-on, who spent most of their time working on their hot rods or at the movies, or—in good weather—on the beaches during the hours allotted to surfing. He knew their names, Otto and Sandy and Grover. They were all staring at him. They were all hostile.

Jose turned back to the warmth and excitement of the ball game, refusing to admit the chill which went through him. He took the heavy bat to the plate to face the redoubtable Jossman, who looked just as unfriendly as Syd and his playmates. He heard Junior barking. He heard the bench begging him to get on base. In fact, he heard everything that went on. His hands were wet with perspiration on the bat handle.

Jossman had the full wind-up, that is, unlike many young pitchers, he threw his leg high, swung his right arm, hiding the ball in his gloved left, turned half away from the plate, then came around and through, all elbows, knees—and blinding speed. The first one went whizzing by Jose as though it had been marked "Express . . . Please Rush."

Jose blinked. In the Little League, the Babe Ruth League and the high school games, all in Los Angeles, he had never seen anything this fast. It was something so new that he became more curious than afraid. He yanked his cap down and squinted at Jossman, watching every move. He tried to sight on the hand holding the ball as soon as it drew back, so that he might possibly catch a glimpse of the pitch from the beginning of its flight.

The Bells pitcher reared back and came through. Keeping a sharp eye on it all the way, Jose stepped in and swung. A curve spun idly away from his bat and he missed it by a foot. The hoots from the visiting players were like banshee howls in Jose's ears.

Catcher Einstein said mockingly, "Now you see it, now you don't," and tossed the ball back to Jossman.

Jose stepped out and patted the dirt from his spikes. He knew he was being overpowered. He reflected, then asked for time. He went to the bat rack and took out his old, thin, light bat. He returned to the batter's box and squared away.

A loud voice yelled, "The greaser couldn't hit a balloon. Stick it in his ears!"

At that moment, Jossman fired a fast ball, using a half

wind-up, a sneaky but fair pitch. Jose, his face burning, swung weakly and fanned out—his first appearance at bat as a Green Soxer.

He walked to the bench, head high, staring at the stands. The voice had come from Syd Grimm's group on the Studio City side. There was some activity there and Mr. Vale moved his tall form through the crowd. Jose kept on going and sat down between a scowling Jack Pilgrim and Aki Matsuo.

"It wasn't Syd," Jack said.

"No, it was not his voice," Aki agreed. He looked puzzled. "Why do they not pick on me?"

Jack asserted, "Nobody's going to pick on anyone if I can help it."

"Leave it alone," Jose begged. "Ignore them."

"Something's got to be done when it comes from our stands, our people."

"It will build and build," said Jose earnestly. "I know. It is better to do nothing, you must believe me."

Mr. Vale was, nevertheless, taking action. He was pointing a finger at someone and the police assigned to the crowd were pushing in that direction.

Then a great howl went up from the people. They were not watching Mr. Vale. They were yelling for a bouncing, giant, furry animal who had broken all restraint and was heading for the Green Sox bench.

Chris Hatfield fell away, staring. Jossman held the ball and gaped. Everybody was howling at once. Junior was on the loose.

Jose came off the bench as though shot from a cannon. He ordered, "Junior! Heel!"

The Saint Bernard put on the brakes. He skidded to a stop in front of the Studio City ball team. Putting his head on one side, he wagged his tail and looked rakishly up and down the line of young players, loving them all.

The cheering was tremendous. Junior wheeled and bobbed his head right and left. Everyone in the park was on his side, it seemed. Coach Johnson heaved a sigh of relief and marched to where Jose was reaching for the dog's collar.

"The excitement in the stands," Jose explained. "It upset him, no? Mama and Papa could not hold him."

Inspired, Johnson said, "Look, do you think he would stay on the sideline? I mean, will he obey me?"

"Oh, he is very obedient . . . sometimes."

"Bring him over. Let's try something."

Jose let go of the dog's collar and walked to the bench. Junior followed in his footsteps, staring amiably around at the Studio City Team. They looked very much alike to him in their green and white uniforms and caps. However, if they were Jose's friends, they were a little bit more than all right in Junior's world.

Coach Johnson was asking the team, "How about Junior for a mascot?"

Harry Keel whooped, "He's my kind of dog. I'm for him."

"He's an infielder," Aki said.

Jack Pilgrim beamed. "Just what we need, Coach."

"He's elected," announced the Coach. "Can you make him stay close to me, Jose?"

Junior flapped an ear. Jose whispered into it, indicating Chuck Johnson. "You want to stay close to me? Then you stick by him—all the time. Be a good dog?"

Junior whimpered assent. He found it very interesting here with the boys, where he could be close to the action. He was a born baseballer. He walked around in a small circle, slurping at each boy in the line. He woofed toward the Cansino family in the stands, to show there were no hard feelings.

Then he went to Chuck Johnson and nudged him in such a friendly fashion that the Coach fell over on the grass. Abashed, he tried to help untangle man and bench. Failing, he sat down, legs slightly askew, and benevolently surveyed this new field of conquest.

Hatfield stood in against the Bells pitcher. The interruption may have jarred the hurler's concentration. At any rate, he threw four wide ones in a row and Hatfield walked. The Green Sox supporters began to shout for blood.

Joe Sampson went to bat and Jack Pilgrim took the on-deck box. Jose sat next to Coach Johnson, and Junior stuck out his tongue and lolled, obviously believing himself the center of attention.

The police were removing Syd Grimm's friends, Otto, Sandy and Grover. Nearby fans had identified Otto as the offender who had gratuitously insulted Jose and his countrymen. Syd was sitting alone, his face red. Everything had a cameolike clarity to Jose, so wrought up was he at this time. He saw Mr. Vale talking with his father and mother and wished the Principal would not be so kind and thoughtful. He only wanted to prove himself on the ball field, to earn his place among his fellow students. He was a new boy and he wanted to be treated as such and left to his own devices.

Joe Sampson exercised his considerable muscle, the bat weaving to and fro like a palm leaf. Jossman took a deep breath, went into his stretch and pitched. It was low and outside and Sampson began to grin. The Bells pitcher seemed to be suffering one of his rare wild spells.

Again Jossman glared at first, toed the rubber and brought his arm over and down. It was called a strike, as this one clipped the outside corner, low and fast. Sampson dug in. Jose watched Jossman with the fascination of a bird held by a snake.

The spell held as the Bells pitcher threw. His pitch had the quickness and sting of the rattler. Sampson, sobered, whiffed the air. Jossman never changed expression—nor did he change his style. The third one came in the spot he had chosen, knee-high on the outer corner.

"Strike three!"

Jack Pilgrim went to face the fire of the Bells star. Jose was off the bench, on one knee, his eyes still glued on Jossman. Jack looked over a ball, then a strike. Then Jossman came through with a curve. The best hitter on the Green Sox, facing the best pitcher of the Bells, snapped his wrists. The bat blurred. The ball went slamming down to short.

Toler, one of the new, tall breed of short fielders, made the stop, snapped it to second. Hatfield, going down with all his might, was out by ten feet.

Jose picked up his glove. He was trying to photograph

Jossman's motion, his style, trying to estimate the speed of the visitor's delivery. It was difficult, to say the least. In position between second and third, Jose thought it out with great care.

Junior, uttering a slight woof, made a small move toward joining his owner on the field. Coach Johnson, not at all sure he would be obeyed, said with what he hoped was calm firmness, "All right, Junior. Stay!"

Junior turned sad brown eyes on the Coach, debated a moment . . . then stayed. Tongue out, he stared at Jose, finally allowing his great round head to drop upon his forepaws as he stretched alongside the Green Sox bench.

Al Birkie did not have the physical equipment of his rival from up the Valley, but he had something else. He had iron nerve and canny control. He went after Sykes, leadoff man in the second, another of the big guns, and made him roll to Aki at second. He found the hard-swinging Anthony had a weakness for close ones and pitched him tight so that he popped to Fred Barker behind the plate. He fed the elongated Toler low curves and saw him go down swinging. The Bells took the field.

Jossman now had recovered his aplomb by now and he was as sharp around the plate as he had been at the start. Harry Keel flied out. Nick Farmer went down on a called third strike. Fred Barker grounded weakly to third, to end the second inning.

Jose was silent, watching from the bench, concentrating, never taking his eye from Jossman. When Junior nosed him, he put a hand on the dog's gigantic, powerful shoulder and absently petted him, but gave him no close attention.

Birkie gave up a hit and a walk in the third, then struck out his pitching opponent, Jossman. Keller, the dangerous leadoff man, was up. Jose and the other infielders increased the tempo of their continual chatter. "Get this one, Al. Easy man, Al. Let's get two here, Al. Throw it past him. We're with you, Al."

Birkie seemed to be made from a solid block of ice. He pitched to Keller as though it were batting practice, keeping the ball low and near or over the plate. The center fielder slapped it hard.

Jose came in, playing the short hop, taking a chance. He got his glove on the ball, swung around. Aki took his toss, jumped high and threw to first. The inning was over on the second double play by the rookie combination of the Green Sox, and the stands roared appreciation.

Jossman, not be to outdone, struck out Aki, then Al Birkie. Jose went up again, still toting his lighter bat. He dug in and fastened his gaze upon Jossman's hand.

A moment later, he popped to right field, a can of corn which came down in Ober's glove. Getting a hit off this Bells hurler was going to be next to impossible, he felt.

No one got on base against Jossman, so Jose came up again in the sixth, with the score still 0 to 0. This time, he came around quicker and topped the ball down to short. Now he had struck out, popped out and grounded out, which was about all he could do without either repeating himself or getting on base.

It went along until the ninth when Birkie faced Sykes,

Anthony and Toler. A glance at the scoreboard showed that Al had given up seven hits in eight innings—but fast fielding and his iron nerve had held the Bells to no score. He threw to Sykes, who grounded out.

He lost Anthony, then, who knocked a single past Jose's desperate, outflung gloved attempt. Toler, who had hit him in the fifth inning and was, like all the Bells, always a threat, came up to try and bunt Anthony along.

Birkie pitched him high, against the bunt. Toler went for it. Anthony took off for second. The ball hit Toler's bat and Jose was already coming in. The little pop was out of Birkie's reach. Jose jumped into the air, grabbed it and, in the same motion, before coming back to earth, flipped it to Harry Keel at first.

Anthony was doubled off as he tried to slide back. The Green Sox raced to the bench. Junior rose to greet them, barking, catching the emotion which filled them as they took their last raps against the favored boys from the upper Valley.

Jossman had, of course, pitched a no-hitter up until now. He had walked only three men. It was Jose's fourth chance against him, leading off, a spot not to be envied. He hesitated, looked at Jack Pilgrim, then took the bigger bat with him, the one with which he had practiced during the past week.

Junior stood, tail erect, ears back. Jose paused to scratch the handsome head. Junior barked at him, as though in encouragement, and the crowd roared.

Jossman was still strong. Jose studied him. If there was a weakness in the Bell pitcher, it was his overweening confidence. Jose stood in there, hoping that he had learned something, hoping he could see just a part of the pitch as it came speeding toward him.

Jossman threw, low and outside, one of his favorite spots, a tough one for any hitter. Jose leaned over and put the fat of the big bat gently against the ball.

Then he ran. Jossman came off the mound, taken by surprise, a little slow. Einstein came out from behind the plate, whipping off his mask. The ball spun and rolled. Jossman picked it up and threw. Jose stomped on first base as the throw arrived.

The umpire seemed to hesitate a fraction of a second, then bawled, "Safe!"

The Bells set up a fearful protest. Junior barked at them, as though backing up the umpire. Jose roosted on the bag and breathed hard, hoping and praying a little. He had indeed learned a lesson—that he might not be able to swing all the way and hit a Jossman pitch, but he could contrive to get a piece of the ball. He had broken up the no-hitter with a bunt single.

Now there was only one thing for Chris Hatfield to do, which was to sacrifice Jose to second. He tried it.

The ball spun down the first-base line. Jossman, no mean fielder, pursued, threw out Chris. But Jose was on second, with one out, Joe Sampson at bat, and Jack Pilgrim coming up next. Coach Johnson flashed a sign and Jose took it, nodding, a little surprised, but agreeable to the decision.

Joe bunted the first pitch. Again, Jossman charged the

ball. Jose was off to a good start. Jossman had to go to first. Jose slid into third.

Two out, and it all rested on Captain Jack Pilgrim's broad and sturdy shoulders. No more sacrifices, not even a long fly, could bring home the winning run. Star pitcher faced star hitter.

Jossman girded himself and threw. One strike.

Jack stepped out, cleaned his spikes, wrapped his hands around the bat and stepped back in the box. Jossman looked at Jose, then threw his best curve, which had kept Jack safe all day long.

The Green Sox captain stepped in. He brought the bat around on a line with the ground and the ball. He met it on the nose. Jose was off like a flash. He knew where that one was going. He danced all the way to the plate, clapping his hands, kicking up his heels. He was yelling and almost weeping as the safe hit went into right field, a mere single, the only real hit off the Bell hurler, but enough to win a ball game.

Junior seemed to know what had happened. He was at home plate, his tail, indeed his entire ample rear end, wagging like a flag in a whipping gale. He almost bowled Jose over, then following him to where his teammates engulfed him, pranced around as though he had won the game for Studio City High all by his dogself.

But it was Jack and Al Birkie who deserved the credit, Jose kept yelling this until he was hoarse. It was the pitching and the beautiful hit in the clutch, not his miserable near-out, he insisted. Nobody seemed in the mood to listen. Everyone was slapping him until he ached and, anyway, there was enough praise and glory to go around, that day.

Junior led the parade to the dressing room. Coach Johnson said, "Bring him in. We'll never let him out of our sight the day of a game. He's our mascot. He gave us a boost."

They had needed a special boost that day—and would need it again when they met the Bells at the end of the season. Jose knew. It was a sobering thought.

6

Syd Grimm's woody was basically a '46 station wagon, completely rebuilt, slightly marred by termites but otherwise snug. It contained beneath the hood an immaculate engine assembled from parts of all vintages—chrome rings, whatever his mechanical ingenuity could contribute within the limits of his pocketbook. He drove to the corner of Curzon and Moorpark to pick up his three friends. It was Sunday morning and overcast not a day for the beach.

Syd was a boy of many moods. His home life was not too happy, since both his father and mother worked at an aircraft plant. Left alone, he was subject to deep and dark depression. He sought companionship among the three high-school dropouts who were also uneasy and not satisfied with the world.

Now, when he saw them on the curbing, sitting in a row, Otto, Sandy and Grover, a thought struck him. They looked somewhat alike, as though they were triplets. Startled, he glanced at himself in the rear-view mirror, to see if he also was one of the adopted family, if he too resembled the others. He was too dark, he thought, with a certain relief; his head was a different shape.

That was not the real difference, however, although he could not know it. The truth was that the three boys on the curbing did not really resemble one another. The similarity lay in their attitudes, in their expressions.

Otto was rather tall and stoop-shouldered, the most muscular of the three. He could have been a good athlete if he had possessed ambition. Sandy was red-haired and wider, with a thick torso and long legs which contrasted oddly. His co-ordination was not very good. Grover, medium-sized, medium-complected, medium everything, had excellent reflexes and had shown promise as a student and a football player, but had lost interest.

That was the trouble with all three of these boys. They had lost interest—in school, in athletics, in just about everything. And Syd Grimm was heading directly along the same path. He swung the woody to the right, pretending that he was going to run down his pals and they stared at him, not moving. He put on the brakes and sat behind the wheel, grinning at them.

Otto said, "Like nothin' man, nothin'."

"Jailbird," jeered Syd. "How come they let you out, man?"

"Like they haven't got a jail big enough," crowed Otto. "My old man, he like to tear down that little old hoosegow they got."

"Gang-busters," agreed Sandy. "Varoom, Otto's out on the street and the fuzz is still screamin'."

Grover laughed. "The fuzz don't like greasers any more than we do, seems like."

The trio rose to their feet and stretched, staring at the sky. Then they got into the station wagon, Otto in front, the other two in the second seat. The third seat had been removed and there were sleeping bags and other objects in the rear. Part of the charm of the old vehicle seemed to be that it was a little home away from home, self-sufficient in emergencies, private and secretive for Syd Grimm and his friends. They kept it polished and free of rust and cracks—except for the trails of the termites. The boys cherished it in an odd, offhand fashion. They even had a name for it among themselves, "The Pirate Den."

Syd drove down Curzon Street, idling, aimless. When boys came to the house on the corner where the Cansino family dwelt, Otto roused himself to glare and mutter, "That greaser kid got me into that trouble."

"Me, too," said Syd. "He got me into plenty of trouble—him and that Jap kid."

"You got to keep your cool, men," cautioned Grover. "You can't go around fightin' City Hall. They got a Reform School for men who lose their cool."

They were all silent at the thought of the correctional institution. Syd turned the corner and they drove slowly past the high fence which restrained Junior from mixing with the neighbors.

Otto said, "That big fat mutt, that's a somethin'."

"Prize dog," Sandy told him. "I had a prize dog once, a Boxer. He ran away, never did find him."

"I'll give him a prize, someday," vowed Otto.

Syd kept on driving. They turned south and went along

a side street lined with eucalyptus trees, tall and straight against the gray sky. There seemed to be nothing attractive in prospect for the day.

Otto grumbled, "Sunday is a washout."

"Why Sunday?"

"No action, man. It's a hang-up," Otto answered impatiently.

But it was because, on weekends, there was no school activity, Syd vaguely knew. His pals had rebelled against school discipline and when classes were out there was nothing for them to fight. They could boo the baseball games and exult in the fact that other kids were studying while they were loafing, but Sunday was empty, useless, because everyone was free on Sunday.

"Where you want to go?" Syd asked.

"Not the beach. I hate gray days at the beach," Sandy answered.

"Downtown?"

"Nothing' but greasers downtown," Otto snarled. "You know better'n that. Your old man told you not to go downtown."

Syd nodded. "That's right, he did. But that's no reason for not goin' if we want to."

"How about San Diego?" asked Sandy. "The zoo."

"Not enough gas," Syd told him. "You got any loot?"

Nobody answered. They had failed to find odd jobs that week, to provide spending money. Their parents had long since cut off their allowances until they should get steady work.

Otto asked, "What's the matter with your dough, Syd? You savin' up for somethin'?"

Syd's eyes suddenly smarted. "My old man's sore about the baseball thing. That I didn't have sense enough to keep my mouth shut."

"I thought he put up an argument, him and your uncles?"

"They argued with Vale, all right. But me, they gave me a hard time. Said I should've laid back and undermined the greaser, the Jap and that Jack Pilgrim."

"Yeah," agreed Otto, "that's what you should've done." He straightened up, his splayed feet pressed against the floorboard. "Hey! I got an idea."

"Like what, man?"

They all brightened. Sunday might not be a waste, after all. Otto, the leader, has an idea!

"Drive back past Cansino's joint."

"What for?"

"We'll take a look, that's what."

With some doubt, Syd wheeled around a corner, headed back to Curzon Street. There was no traffic, and he turned at the next corner and again they surveyed the high wall. The house seemed deserted.

"Gone to church," Otto guessed. "Park over there. Keep the engine runnin'."

He got out, a big boy, blond and freckled. He strolled across the street. Sandy and Grover joined him, a step or two to the rear. Syd remained in the car.

Otto estimated the height of the wall, said, "Gimme a foot up."

Grover laced his hands together. Otto put a toe in the arch of the proffered grip, leaped, caught the top of the fence.

"No barbed wire or nothin'," he called. "C'mon."

"What's the idea?"

"Never mind. Come on up, one of you."

Sandy obeyed. Grover tried to jump and catch the top of the fence and failed. Otto looked into the well-kept yard. He considered.

"We get caught up here, we're in trouble," said Sandy uneasily.

"Why? We're just visitin' our buddy Jose, aren't we? Hey, look at the rosebushes."

Mama Cansino was very proud of her roses. She had purchased them from a drugstore chain at a sale and people had told her they would not blossom. By careful care and much watering she had brought them to full and lovely bloom. They were red and white and yellow, all in a row.

"Nice," said Sandy.

"What if they got torn up? Maybe that big mutt would get blamed for it," suggested Otto.

"Why tear up roses?" Sandy was not comfortable on the top of the fence. He looked up and down the quiet street.

"Nobody's around," Otto said. "The dog'll get a beatin' if they think he did it, won't he?"

"I wouldn't want the job of whippin' him."

From the ground, Grover called, "Either do somethin' or knock it off. This is no fun."

Otto laughed, a high, jarring note. "Chicken, you're all chicken."

He dropped into the yard and started for the rose garden, looking for an implement to attack the bushes. He found a sharp stick and went to the end, where a cluster of deep red roses proudly raised their heads. He lifted the stake and was about to plunge it into the soft earth.

There was a low growl. Sandy yelled, "Look out!"

Junior had been taking a nap. He knew about Sunday— that everyone went away for a while and then came back and spent a lot of time with him. He was willing to wait, dozing comfortably in the shade of a lilac bush, unnoticed, dreaming of platters of dog food and a happy Jose on this special day.

When he saw Otto, he was puzzled. It took a moment to shake off slumber. Then he noticed the stick and thought that the nice stranger was going to play with him. It was no more than polite to let out a pleased sound, an indication that he was ready for fun.

The next move was to run, so that he could grab the end of the stick in his teeth. This was not a throwing stick, he knew. It was a tugging stick. He would worry one end while the visitor tried to hold onto the other. Very few people could wrestle a stick away from Junior, once he got a grip on it.

It seemed strange that the nice boy just stood there staring, while the other boy on the fence shouted. This was not Sunday behavior. People were usually quieter and happier on Sunday after they came home from wherever they went. The thing to do, Junior decided, was to encourage the boy in the yard to play the game.

The way to do this was to run. If a dog got up a good rate of speed, he could snatch at the stick as he went by. Then the boy would pull it back. Junior didn't mind missing a couple of times. It prolonged the fun. If he could just run fast enough, the boy might appreciate his attitude and then everything would be fine.

Otto stood frozen for a moment. Sandy was howling, "He'll tear you to pieces. Run, Otto, run!"

Otto looked wildly around. He had not thought about an avenue of retreat. He had forgotten that he could not get over the fence without help. The huge animal was charging him.

He dropped the stick—it was no weapon against an angry beast of this size. He began to run, although he did not know where he was going. The yard was large, but not big enough to get to a safe spot. He ran toward the house, doubled in his tracks and charged blindly back, scared out of his wits.

Junior had stopped to pick up the stick. If there was a variation of the game, he was going to go along with it. Any kind of play was better than no play.

Otto was gibbering with fear. "I can't get out! Get me out, Sandy!"

"The gate, the gate," Sandy yelled. "Over there, see it?"

Otto could see nothing but the Saint Bernard. Junior had the stick in his mouth and was lumbering toward him. Otto ran again.

Junior loped along behind. Each time he caught up, he slowed down, growling to show how pleased he was. Oddly, the boy merely turned and scuttled in another direction. It was like a game of tag, only the stranger didn't seem to understand the finer points.

Up and down they went on the grass. Twice Otto

slipped and nearly fell. His breath was coming faster and faster. He was running out of wind.

"The gate, the gate!" Sandy kept yelling, but Otto could not locate the gate.

In the street, Grover was asking, "What's going on in there, anyway? What's the matter with Otto?"

"The dog's trying to kill him!" yelled Sandy.

Grover turned and shouted to Syd, "The dog's tryin' to eat Otto."

Syd got out of his car and ran across the street. "Put me up there," he told Grover.

Atop the fence, alongside of Sandy, he saw the predicament at once. He said, "This way, Otto."

The big boy looked up, terrified, panting. "He's goin' to get me!"

"To your right," Syd directed him. "Straight down the yard."

Otto blindly obeyed. Junior trotted after him.

"There's a bolt, see it? Pull the bolt."

Otto grabbed, missed. Junior was almost on top of him. He could feel those fangs tearing at his flesh.

Junior dropped the stick and looked interested. Was the new boy going to open the gate? He shouldn't do that on this day. Any other day and Junior knew where to find Jose. But on this day he stayed home and waited and everything worked out fine.

Otto's shaky fingers finally found the bolt and drew it. He yanked open the gate, shot through and into the street. Syd dropped down to earth and went to the gate and closed it. Otto was already in the car and the other two were piling in behind him.

Syd waited a moment. The dog made no attempt to chase after Otto. His small, whining call did not seem to be fearsome. Syd walked across the street and got behind the wheel.

"Get us out of here," Otto babbled. "Did you see him, Sandy? He was tryin' to kill me."

Sandy observed, "I dunno. He caught up to you a couple of times, but he didn't jump on you."

"He was playin' with me. Like the cat plays with a mouse. Did you see those teeth? He was goin' to tear me limb from limb."

As Syd drove away from the curb, he asked quietly, "You don't know much about dogs, do you, Otto?"

"I hate 'em. I hate all mutts." Otto was shaking as though he had chills and fever.

"Saint Bernards won't attack anybody," Syd told him. "They're not vicious."

"Not vicious? Are you nuts or somethin'?"

"No use trying to explain if you're afraid of dogs," said Syd. "It happens to be the truth, though."

Otto inhaled deeply. The silence of the other two boys indicated that he had lost face. He had to regain his position of authority some way. After a moment, he was able to laugh. "Is that a fact? A bug mutt like that, he wouldn't hurt anybody?"

"Only if he jumps on you in fun. He's so big, naturally he could knock you down."

Otto said, "I never knew that. Say, that's somethin' to

know." He pretended cheerfulness. "Sure fooled me. Had me goin' there, for a minute or two."

"Sure did," said Sandy. "Goin' up and down that yard."

"Hey, the sun's comin' out," Otto cried. "The beach, men. Let's get the boards and go surfin'."

Otto was a real hot dog on a surfboard, by far the best of the four of them. Once down at the oceanside, he could quickly assume superiority again. Syd thought about this, but let it go.

After all, these were his only buddy-buddies, now. He'd been fired from the baseball team. He was thinking about quitting school. He needed friends.

Back in the Cansino yard, Junior surveyed the gate. He could open it with ease if he tried. It was a question of whether it would be any fun. The strange boy had quit in such a hurry that it was doubtful there would be any more running games. The sun was coming through and it would be getting warm.

Junior decided it wasn't worth the trouble. He picked up the stick, worried it awhile. Then he went back to his place in the shade. It had been fun, no question about that. New games were a bit hard to understand and the boy had made quite a lot of noise about it, but he had made the best of it.

The Saint Bernard was dreaming of cats, his nose twitching, when Jose came home, found the gate unlocked and wondered how Junior could possibly have managed it.

Jack Pilgrim sat in Coach Chuck Johnson's office and
stared at the official scorebook which contained a full ac-
count of last Saturday's game with the Bellingham Bells.
It was Monday afternoon and the squad was out on the
field going through their paces.

"We were lucky," he remarked. "But we won, didn't
we?"

"You stayed in there and Cansino bunted us to glory,"
agreed the Coach. "Jossman is a terrific pitcher, but not
that good. We've got a problem, Jack. I want the boys
to work on hitting, but we've also got to run and take
chances and strengthen our defense."

"Nothing wrong with the outfield," said Jack. "You're
worrying about the kids, aren't you?"

"Cansino and Matsuo? Yes, a little. They did a fine job
Saturday. Can they keep it up under pressure? It's not fair
to ask too much of them."

"I think they'll field as well or better than Cohen and Grimm. Their hitting—that's another matter. Young kids have trouble with the bat unless they're naturals."

"Next Saturday it's South Hollywood," Johnson reminded him. "They have a fair pitcher in Stack. They shine with the bat. They'll hit Birkie. They love his style. What about Hunter?"

"He needs to lose five pounds," admitted Jack. "He'll have to run a lot."

"He'll have to do push-aways from the dinner table," suggested Johnson.

"He likes to eat—ice cream and cake."

"Me, too," said Johnson surprisingly. "I have a terrible time resisting."

They laughed together. There was a fine understanding between them as they walked to the practice field. Jack felt lucky to be playing for the Studio City High coach.

He paused to watch Jose in the batting cage. The kid tried very hard to remember everything that had been told him. Tod Hunter, perspiring profusely, was throwing hard. Jose was attempting to hit to all fields, according to where the ball was pitched. He was not succeeding very well.

Then his turn was completed and he took a practice bunt, as was required. He dragged the ball perfectly, ran down to first. It would have been a hit in any real game.

Jack turned and saw Johnson looking significantly at him. Cansino might never be a slugger, but he would remain in the leadoff position because of his ability to lay one down and his speed afoot.

Aki Matsuo was a different problem. He was in there now, and it was terribly plain that he was off stride. Johnson went to him and took the bat and began to talk slowly and with great care.

"On balance, Aki. You're jumping at the ball. We don't want home runs from you."

Aki's brown eyes opened wide.

Johnson went on, "In fact, I am ordering you not to hit a homer."

Everyone within hearing guffawed and Aki showed his white teeth in a rueful grin and said, "Not likely, sir."

"What I want from you is a life—a well-placed dinky hit that'll put you on base. After the next man, our sterling pitcher, whoever he might be, strikes out, we have Cansino. Now I don't want any long balls from him, either. Bad for his system. If there are not two outs, he will bunt and you will go to second. Then we have hitters coming up. Understand?"

Aki said humbly, "Only too well, sir. I will do my best. I'm afraid I'm what they call 'good field, no hit.'"

"Maybe you are, right now," Johnson told him, "but stick around and we'll see that you improve."

Aki went back to work, but his efforts were far from remarkable. Jack Pilgrim agreed that the coach was right, there were problems. They had nine games to play before meeting the Bells again in the crucial game. There must be a general improvement in the batting. Four long-ball hitters did not make a ball club.

He went out to the field and began shagging fly balls. He ran as fast as he could, and when Birkie took over the batting practice pitching job, he made Tod Hunter run behind him, matching every step he took.

"I'm tired," complained the roly-poly boy.

"You want to eat cake and ice cream? Then you'll have to run it off every afternoon. Take your choice."

Tod thought it over. Then he said, "I'll take the dessert. Runnin's good for my legs, any old way."

"And Birkie will pitch all the important games," Jack warned him.

"Well, he's smarter'n I am," Tod reasoned. "I just throw the ball."

"You throw it mighty hard," Jack told him. "Now, will you peel off some pounds and get ready?"

Tod sighed. "I'll try, but I'm not very strong when I see cake and ice cream." He paddled off.

Coach Johnson was setting the infield defense and motioning to Jack that he wanted the team to try the cutoff plays. It wasn't exciting, really, but it was part of the workload which was necessary if Studio City was going to have a successful season.

It was odd about Tod Hunter, Jack thought. Beneath the considerable blubber there was a strong, stocky boy with plenty of natural pitching ability. If Tod had half of Jose Cansino's ambition, he would be the ace hurler of the team.

Jose Cansino was taking Jack's throw from the outfield grass, relaying it to home plate under the coach's direction. He was plotting the proper cutoff from the outfield in his mind, according to how many were on base and what bases they occupied. These things, he knew, had to

become automatic. There wasn't time to think them out
when a game was in progress. Baseball at its best had to
be a game of reflexes, and the man who acted smoothly
and promptly was often a game saver in a clutch situation.

Aki seemed to have it all down pat. He was small and
his arm wasn't the best or strongest, but he got the ball off
so quickly it did not matter. If Aki could begin to hit . . .
Well, if Jose began to hit, also . . . there was a chance for
the championship. It depended upon the two of them, a
fact which was beginning to haunt him. He well knew the
old baseball saying, "A hero one day, a bum the next." It
could happen to him.

He missed a throw-in, just thinking about it, and Coach
Johnson called, "Pay attention, Cansino."

It was going to be that kind of a week. There was a
letdown after the narrow victory over the Bells. It was not
that the team was overconfident; quite the contrary. Re-
membering how it had happened, they were conscious of
how good fortune had attended them. They began trying
very hard, and by Friday they were stale. They were
pressing.

Coach Johnson knew it. He gave them Friday afternoon
off. He told them, "Take it easy, do whatever you want.
Make sure you are up in your classes, that's all I ask. On
Saturday, we face the big bombers. Forget it. Just relax
and you'll feel better about everything."

He hoped he was correct.

Syd Grimm had been sitting across the street all week,
in the station wagon, watching the practice. Otto was

barred from the school premises because of the incident of the previous week, but he and the other two sat with Syd, having nothing else in particular to do.

Syd said, "Well, that goes to show it was a flash in the pan against the Bells. They haven't got it. They just can't make it without Cohen and me."

"Yeah, big deal." Otto yawned. "So what? You're fired and the greaser gets to play. Win or lose, you're out, he's in."

Syd drove off toward the beach, silent, stewing in his mind. He would never admit it, but he would far rather be playing baseball than hanging around trying to find occupation for his time and that of his three companions.

Jose spent Friday afternoon with Junior. "If you're going to be a mascot, you have to be shiny, *amigo*," he decided.

This required much exertion. Junior did not like to be curried and combed and brushed. It was hardly necessary to give him a bath; Jose had only to play the garden hose and he would take a shower with glee, especially if he thought Jose was trying to avoid spraying him.

There was much loud canine noise that afternoon. Finally, Jose gave up, deciding that Saturday morning, when the butterflies were active in his middle, would be a better time to make Junior presentable.

Somehow or other, Jack Pilgrim could not get away from Lion that same afternoon. The big cat was waiting for him at the bicycle stand, mewing in his hoarse voice, rubbing hard against Jack's ankles, demanding attention.

Even the cat's nervous, Jack thought. "Are we going to get our lumps tomorrow, old monster?"

"Meow, *grrrr*," said Lion. It did seem that he was trying to tell Jack something.

Aki came by and paused to look at the captain of the team and the huge feline. "Maybe he is jealous because Junior was picked to be the mascot."

Jack looked startled. "You think he knows?"

"Cats are very sensitive creatures," said Aki. "I have two at home."

"You do? Two?"

"Two tomcats, but smaller than Lion. Brothers. They are very intelligent. They answer to their names. They play games. And they always want their own way."

"Proud," said Jack. "Old Lion, he's very proud."

"Oriental people are very fond of cats and respectful toward them, too," Aki observed. He bent down and scratched Lion's head between the ears. The big creature purred.

"He won't let most people near him," Jack said.

"They know their friends." Aki did not smile. "Are you concerned about the game tomorrow?"

"Well, those guys hit control pitching real good," answered Jack. "We'll have to get a lot of runs to beat 'em. Birkie's their dish of tea."

"And Tod isn't ready."

"How can you tell about a butterball like Tod? He's a real nice kid, but he's kind of nutty."

"Flaky?" suggested Aki.

"That's what they call 'em," Jack agreed. "Flaky. It's not easy to tell about kids like Tod."

Aki said, "If Jose and I can only get on base." He blinked. "It's hard not to worry."

"Go home and take it easy, like Coach said." Jack tried to give the little second baseman an encouraging grin. "If we can beat the Bells, we can beat 'em all."

Aki went off on a dog trot. Lion sent a loud cry after him, as though he knew all about it and did not want his friends to worry.

Jack mounted his bike and rode home. He had played against the South Hollywood Suns, so he knew what to expect. Thunder and lightning were in their bats.

Coach Chuck Johnson was explaining this to Principal Vale, who listened attentively. "They're sluggers. No finesse, but they really powder the ball."

"Yes, so I remember from last year," said the dignified educator, himself a baseball fan of the first rank. "Our boys are rather on the weak side, are they not?"

"We have four big bombers. They also strike out a lot," said Coach Johnson moodily.

"Er, Syd Grimm was a good hitter, was he not?"

"Yes, he was strong."

"I'm worried about that boy. His associations are not good," declared Mr. Vale. "They have not been able to learn who set off the fire alarms, you know. Were those three, the dropouts, in the neighborhood at the time?"

"I really don't know. I don't quite believe Syd would do a thing like that, sir."

"A dog is known by the company he keeps. By the way, that Saint Bernard keeps good company."

"Well, thank you, sir."

"It was a very wise move to induct him as mascot. The Cansino boy is excellent in his studies. Too bad he isn't a hitter."

"He'll give everything he has to give," promised the Coach.

"Angels can do no more," said Mr. Vale, smiling. "I'll be there tomorrow, needless to say. Wish I could pinch-hit."

He grasped an imaginary bat and flexed his muscles.

"I didn't know you played ball, sir."

The Principal drew himself up to his full six feet. "I batted .354 my last year in college, Mr. Johnson. And played errorless ball in the outfield . . . well, er . . . almost I do remember a fly ball which rather got lost in the sun. . . . But never mind that. Good luck tomorrow. I hope we outscore those slugging Suns."

"Yes, sir," said Chuck Johnson, leaving the office.

There wasn't much chance, he thought, of outscoring the South Hollywoods. Birkie just didn't have the speed to keep them off balance, a matter proven last year when he had been knocked out of the box in the third inning.

8

Junior did not object in the least to Jose's brushing and fussing on Saturday morning. It was as if he knew that this was a gala event, his first full-time appearance as the mascot of the Green Sox baseball team.

Jose told him, "And it could be the last. We are not so hopeful today."

This did not affect Junior's happiness and pride. He ducked his head for the slip-chain attached to the strong leash and walked with head high, lifting his big pads like a circus horse on parade as he walked with Jose to the school ball field, along Curzon Avenue.

They turned in at the gate, now opened to them by one of the policemen, who grinned and patted Junior's massive head. They went toward the locker room—and were suddenly confronted by the biggest cat Junior had ever seen, as Lion barred their way.

It so happened that Lion, on his part, had never seen

such a large dog, either. At least he had not seen Junior up close, where he could really judge his size.

The cat backed up a step. His fur stood up like the quills of a porcupine. Hissing, spitting, he backed still another pace or two.

Junior lowered his head and whimpered a little. He did not understand instant hostility. After all, he hadn't done anything to this feline. He couldn't very well give chase, since this was an occasion demanding good behavior— and because he was on that choke leash which Jose held very firmly indeed. He lolled out his tongue and looked quite sad.

Jose said, "Lion, this dog is your friend. Do you not understand? Junior would not hurt a cat. He would not even hurt a flea, in case you have fleas. Go away if you are going to behave like that."

Just then, Jack Pilgrim parked his Chevy at the curbing and came through the gate, calling, "Lion won't hurt him. Here, Lion. Come on, I brought you liver."

Lion made one last spitting sound and paddled rearward to the end of the grandstand, never taking his eyes from Junior. Then he vanished.

"Like the Cheshire cat in *Alice and Wonderland,* he just disappeared," said Jack.

"Junior is very friendly, believe me," Jose pleaded.

"I know, but Lion's not used to giants," Jack told him. Let's go. Lion can take care of himself, believe *me.*"

They went into the locker room. The boys were dressing. Coach Johnson was in his office. It was uneasily quiet. There was no joking or laughing.

Then Junior came among them. He went to each player individually, lapping at them all with his big tongue, pawing at them, making dog sounds. He went back and began all over again, missing no one.

The coach came out and Junior went plunging at him, with Jose still holding onto the leash to keep the dog from trampling the man with love.

Johnson said, "Now, Junior, down, boy. Mustn't jump on people, you know."

Someone called, "You scared of him, Coach?"

Laughter swept the room as Junior managed to get his forelegs on Chuck Johnson's hips and cling tight as he attempted to lick the Coach's face. Jose got hold of the collar and talked, but Junior hung on.

Then Johnson began to laugh, too, and the atmosphere of the room because entirely different. Junior calmed down and sat in a corner, his tongue hanging out the side of his mouth, one ear cocked, enjoying it all.

The boys finished dressing quickly and then there was a general discussion about how to make their entry upon the field. The stands were only partially filled, but the squad wanted to do it up right. It was finally decided that Jack Pilgrim should take Junior's leash, as captain, and lead them all out in triumph.

That was the way they planned it, anyway. Jack gingerly took hold of the leather strap. The team lined up and was ready. Jose gave Junior a boost at the doorway. The Saint Bernard got the idea that it was a race. He took off. Jack, unaccustomed to yanking tight on the chain and fearful of hurting the dog, was hauled into view with startling suddenness. The team began to call advice and Jose had to speed up, pass Jack and grab for the collar. . . . Junior just jumped around. Jack let go of him. Jose dragged their mascot to the bench. Now everyone was laughing.

Coach Johnson came over, and Junior immediately went into his act. He knew who was boss by now and he intended giving his all for the Coach. Jose got him attached to a special spike driven into the end of the bench, and he sat down and beamed upon one and all.

Jose gave him a briefing, "Now you mind the Coach, or I will take you back home. You want to go back home?"

Junior did not want to go anywhere.

"All right, then, you will behave yourself." Jose rattled off some Spanish, which always scared the dog a bit, since it was in this language that he got his worst scoldings.

Jose sighed and went out to take practice. It was then he saw the South Hollywood boys for the first time. They were all about eight feet high, he thought. On second look, they were merely six feet tall—all of them. Coach Tom Fall had fallen heir to a bunch of huskies who just happened to be around, ready to play ball, at the same time.

Some of them were quick, too. Acker, their rangy first baseman, was as fast as the shortstop, Norris, who was the one-hundred-yard-dash champion.

It was a sober bunch of Green Sox who gathered for last-minute instructions before taking the field. The coach merely told them, "Bear down every minute and don't let them run wild. That's all."

Al Birkie seemed terribly small on the pitcher's mound facing Acker. It was most unusual for a first-sacker to be leading off, Jose thought, but all the Suns were dangerous in any spot. Birkie wound up and let fly.

Acker bunted down the first-base line, dragging it, then outlegging it as Birkie came over and Fred Barker scrambled from behind the plate. Neither could make the play and Acker was safe.

Birkie mumbled to himself and went back to position.

Jose chirped, "Okay, Al, let's get two, now. Let's go, now."

Aki and the other infielders joined in. Birkie, scowling, faced Ober, the Sun's right fielder, checked the runner and threw his best curve.

Ober swung like a Ted Williams. The ball shot between first and second. Aki flew over but could not get a glove on it. Jose nacked him up, but there were men on first and second.

Up to the plate came Calvin, a great long-ball hitter. There was nothing for Birkie to do but keep the ball low and on the outside, hoping to make the batter knock it on the ground to the infield.

Calvin had other ideas. He golfed one into left field. By the time Sampson had picked it up, Acker had scored, Ober was on third and Calvin was on first base.

On the bench, Coach Johnson said to Tod Hunter, "Go to the bullpen and warm up with young Byron. I just hope you skipped dessert last night."

"Well, no, I didn't," confessed Tod. He brightened. "But I didn't have either cake or ice cream today, sir!"

"Marvelous," said Johnson with sarcasm. Just get ready. Al isn't having a nice afternoon."

Mount, a giant left fielder, was batting. Birkie got a strike on him, then missed with two, then came in with his curve again. Mount slammed it at Aki, a real grass-cutter that amost handcuffed the second sacker.

Aki hung on, made a cop and tossed to Jose, who touched second base and slammed it to first. Harry had to reach a little, but the double play was completed—as Ober went in to count another run for South Hollywood.

Now there were two out and the bases were clean. Birkie could work with comparative confidence, Jose thought. The hitter was Kelly, third base, a very strong boy.

Birkie took his full wind-up. He threw his best slider. It hung, just a little.

Kelly knocked it over the fence.

Jose watched the ball go far over Jack Pilgrim's head. It was a sad sight. Three runs in the first inning and it was all too plain that Birkie couldn't handle these sluggers. How would Studio City ever get back into this game, he wondered?

Harder, the second baseman, was up. Birkie gritted his teeth and tossed another curve. Harder hit into it and the ball came down like a bullet to shortstop.

Jose charged it. He snatched it on the first bounce. He snapped off his throw as Harder sped to first. He beat the Sun runner by ten feet. The inning for the visitors was over at last. They had racked up four hits and three runs off Al Birkie.

Jose took the bigger bat and went to the plate. Now the Studio City team saw that Coach Fall had a surprise for them. On the mound was a new boy, named Cy Seidman. He had the height and the long arms of a basketball player—which he was. He had a wide grin and a windmill style of pitching, all elbows and knees.

Jose waited in the batter's box. It seemed that the Sun thrower could take a step and stick the ball directly into Catcher Solvo's mitt.

Seidman wound up and threw. Jose got a glimpse of the stitches on this one. He leveled off on it, brought the bat smoothly around and let the speed of the pitch do the work for him. He heard the satisfactory spat of leather on wood and set sail. He went down to first like a runaway express on an open track.

The ball was bouncing into right field. Sampson was bringing his bat to the plate. The stands were yelling for blood. Junior was woofing away at his end of the bench.

Jose was more surprised than pleased. The Sun hurler had thrown the ball very hard. He evidently was a speed specialist that Coach Fall hoped would blind the opposition.

Sampson stood in there, a bit pigeon-toed, not a graceful looking boy. Seidman scowled over at Jose and then threw another hard one.

Sampson hit it right on the nose. It was dropping sharply into left field when Jose slowed to make sure it would not be caught.

Then he was running like a ghost. He saw that the ball had slid past Mount. He headed for third and got down and threw himself through the dust.

He heard the third-base coach yelling, "Get up and run, you clown! Run!"

Mount had not yet picked up the ball. Jose took a deep breath and set sail for home. He made it easily as Sampson held up at second with a lucky double.

Coach Johnson said, "Nice going, Jose."

"I should not have slid into third."

"You got up, didn't you? We have one of the runs back. This Seidman boy has speed, now let's see about his aim."

Chris Hatfield was at bat. The Seidman boy surveyed him with fierce eyes and began to pitch. He struck out Chris, made Jack Pilgrim foul out, and then he fanned Harry Keel. He was throwing pitches that looked like a beebee shot.

"Cansino and Sampson made him mad," said Coach Johnson wonderingly. "He can really throw hard!"

Junior, his only audience, said, "*Woof*," in subdued accents and ceased to wag his tail.

Al Birkie faced the tail end of the battering order. Norris, the track star at shortstop, promptly lined a grounder to deep short. Jose trapped the ball and made one of his clothesline, quick throws, then stood there, blinking, disbelieving. Norris had beat it out for a safety.

Solvo, the catcher, came up next. Birkie tried to keep the ball down low but got it nearly waist-high. Solvo hit it deep into right field and Hatfield began to run. Norris held up a moment, then took off.

Hatfield never did catch up to that one. It just kept sailing, over the trees and far away. Coach Johnson got up off the bench. Junior started to go with him, but stopped at the end of his chain, head down, dejected.

Up in the stands, high above everyone watching, Lion arched his back, yawned and went to sleep.

The coach was talking to Birkie. "You're not having a nice afternoon, Al."

Birkie said, "They like me. They like me real good."

"The pitcher is next. Think you can handle him?"

Jose, Aki, Nick and Harry Keel were all gathered around the hill. Birkie looked at them and wiped his streaming brow.

"I couldn't handle Mickey Mouse. I couldn't strike out Charlie Brown. But who's going to do anything about these Sun boys?"

"Maybe nobody," replied Johnson. "Try and get Seidman out, Birkie."

"Oh, I'll try. I'm a big giver," said Birkie, disguising his bitterness beneath a small grin.

Johnson plodded away. Birkie sighed and took the mound. Back of the stands, Tod Hunter was staring, open-mouthed, at the coach's approach.

Tod said, "Yes, sir. I get the message, sir. I'm the next victim."

"How's your control?"

"Ask him," answered Tod, indicating young Byron.

Jay blushed as usual and said, "He's hitting the corners, Coach. Look." He held up his left hand. It was slightly swollen and quite red.

"Just lay it to them." A shout went up as Seidman

swung like a woman softball player and was out on strikes.

"Right now?" Tod was frightened.

"Not tomorrow," Johnson snapped. "Haul yourself out there and pitch."

Tod tossed the ball to Jay and shambled around the end of the stands and toward the mound. The home-town crowd was silent, horrified at the sudden onslaught of the Suns. Five to one, with one out in the second inning—and the Green Sox going against a speed-ball artist, it was enough to send the fainthearted fans toward home for an afternoon barbecue. Mr. Vale stood up and ordered the cheer leaders, "Let's hear it for Birkie, then for Hunter."

Unlike the East and other sections of the United States baseball and other sports offer a good excuse for cheer leaders and even a band—not just football.

There wasn't much optimism in the cheer, but it rose bravely on the afternoon air. Tod took the ball from Birkie. For a moment it seemed they would weep on each other's shoulders, then Birkie went to the bench and donned a windbreaker and Hunter took his allotted warmup.

The Sun coaches were cavorting at first and third, mockingly asserting that victim number two would fare no better than number one, exhorting Acker to lean hard on this one, counting their victory with total glee.

Jose stood alongside Tod Hunter. "You all right, no?"

"I'm scared silly." The stout boy looked straight at the shortstop. "Hey, just keep nailin' those grass-cutters. We won't run off the field yet."

There was a strange glint in Hunter's eyes. Jose suddenly felt a lot better. Beneath the blubber there was a heart which beat strongly, he perceived.

"Stuff it down their throats, no?"

"Be hopeful," said Tod.

He faced the graceful Acker, his shirt slightly rumpled at his ample waist, his shoulders drooping. Tod did not believe in elaborate wind-ups. His style, or lack of it, was just to throw the ball. He nodded at Barker's sign for the fast ball, leaned back and threw with what appeared to be ordinary effort.

The ball almost vanished. Acker, a graceful man, stood flatfooted, his eyes large and round as the umpire bawled, "Stuh—rike!"

A moment later it was "Stuh—rike t'ree, yer *out*."

Acker hadn't moved his bat. He walked away, muttering to himself. Ober came up.

Tod blinked owlish eyes at Jose, then at the other infielders. His soft mouth was suddenly very firm and it occurred to Jose that he looked as he might when he would be a grownup, years from now.

Ober, a calm boy, waited out two pitches. Both were low and inside, but both caught the corners. The next one seemed to come right down the middle, and the right fielder of the Suns stepped into it with all his considerable might. The ball rose like a swallow over the bat.

He missed by a few inches. He gazed at his bat as though it had a hole in it. Then he threw it away and looked for his glove, which he carried to the outfield as though it were a fragile piece of china. Ober wasn't sure he had been seeing straight.

On the Green Sox bench it was somewhat quiet. The other players just looked at Tod, who was sitting with his head down, quite as though he had been knocked out of the box. Coach Johnson made a sign, and none of his teammates went near the pitcher.

Jack Pilgrim whispered, "Is he for real?"

Johnson whispered back, "The Suns think so."

Seidman, however, picked up where he had left off. He made Nick Farmer pop out. Fred Barker grounded weakly to short and poor Aki struck out on three swift pitches.

Tod shucked his windbreaker and took a deep breath. His chubby features were serene, unsmiling. He walked out to the pitcher's mound, gripped a baseball, and began to throw. With each ball Coach Johnson stirred a little on the bench. Alongside him, Junior did the same, adding a little woof of joy.

It was up to the Sun batters to hit the ball. Tod was threading the needle every time he threw. His odd little motion, his quickness, had them off balance. They were big, strong boys and therefore just a trifle muscle-bound. They could wait out the curve ball, pick on the change-up. They had a good eye for the errant pitch. But they simply had never seen anything like Tod's performance.

He got Calvin. He made Mount fly out. He struck out Kelly, the home-run hitter. He walked off with his head a little higher, sat down, looked around and exhaled.

"*Whoosh!*" he puffed. "It's workin' for me."

"What's working for you?" asked Coach Johnson.

"Layin' off ice cream and cake today."

"Oh . . . that!" It was better not to comment further. It was best to hold his breath, Chuck Johnson decided. The score was still five to one. There was nothing to be very happy about.

Tod suddenly realized he was the hitter. He selected a bat at random and waddled to the plate. The Sun players were on him, yelling and deriding him as "the fat boy," and having a lot of fun. He made them feel good by feebly waving at three swift ones to make the first out.

Jose, with the big bat, was at the platter next. He knew that he had to pick up the ball as it left Seidman's hand. He ignored the weird, flapping motion of the South Hollywood pitcher with an effort, straining his eyes. He let the first one go and it was a ball.

Well, he had seen it all the way. He shortened his grip on the bat and crouched a little. Seidman waggled his elbow, his ears, and threw up a long leg. He came over and down with all his speed.

Jose remembered his lesson. He brought the bat around on that level parallel to the ground. He met the ball and sprinted. He may not have been quite as swift as Norris, but he was down to first before the throw from third baseman Kelly arrived.

Sampson walked up with vengeance in his eye. He let Seidman throw two. Then he bunted.

Jose was off with the motion of the pitcher. The ball squirmed on the first-base line. Sampson beat it out by a scant inch.

Hatfield, another right-hand hitter, was next. Seidman

squinted at second, at first. He moistened his dry lips. He went into his check motion.

It occurred to Jose that Seidman needed his windmill style to get the ball where he wanted it. With men on the bases, he was not so sure of his control.

The pitch went in, a bit outside, not a good one. It happened to be in Hatfield's groove. He met it on the end of his bat. It went humpbacked into right field and Jose was sprinting past third and on his way home.

Ober came in to grab the ball. He leaned back and threw for the plate with all his strength. Jose slid along the path, hooked around Solvo and dented the plate. Sampson went to third and Hatfield to second. Now it was five to two and none out and Jack Pilgrim coming to the war.

Jack gripped the same bat Jose had used, with a difference. He held it at the extreme end. Jack was going for the route.

On the bench, Jose was excitedly telling the Coach, "Mr. Johnson, I think Seidman does not like men on the bases, no? Recovering himself, he went on, "Did you notice? He's wild when someone is on, is he not?"

"I noticed," replied Johnson. "And that's good observation, Jose. I've already spoken to the others."

Junior was leaping at the end of his chain and it was necessary for Jose to sit beside him. They both watched Jack Pilgrim. The count was now three and two.

Seidman looked at the base runners, took a deep breath and threw the ball. Jack was dug in, his spikes gripping the dirt. All his strength went into the swing.

There was a loud cracking sound. The ball took off like

an eagle in full flight. The runners took one look at Ober as he ran, then began dancing toward home.

It was debatable which ball had gone farther, Ober's or Jack's, but it didn't matter. Jack trotted around and the score was tied at five all. The stands came alive with loud and constant cheering. Lion woke up and began licking himself. Junior bounced around like a small and cheerful elephant.

And Seidman proceeded to strike out Harry Keel and Nick Farmer, now that the bases were empty, to retire the side. He had given up four hits and four runs . . . and had made three Green Sox fan!

"You should not hit the home run. We should always have someone on base, no?" Jose suggested to Jack as they took the field.

"We should always be so lucky as to find a Tod Hunter," replied Jack. "How about that fat little guy?"

At their side, Aki remarked, "To me he doesn't look so little. He looks ten feet high!"

They took their positions.

There was not another hit on either side throughout the game until the end of the eighth inning. Seidman was invincible with no one on base. Tod Hunter never let a Sun player get to first base with his pinpoint speed pitches. It was still a tie score at five apiece when Jose came up to lead off the last part of the next to the last canto.

Across the street in his station wagon, Syd Grimm sighed. Otto, Grover and Sandy were sprawled there with him, sneering at the Green Sox ballplayers, making remarks that they thought were funny. Somehow or other,

Syd could not join in. Much as he despised Jose, he found himself secretly rooting for the leadoff man to get to first base.

Seidman was not arm-weary; he seemed stronger than when he started. His long limbs windmilled, he threw with tremendous speed. Jose was taut as a bowstring, his eye on the flight of the ball.

Perhaps Seidman was too cautious with the hitter who had twice begun the rallies which tied up the ball game. At any rate, the first two pitches missed the plate.

Then Jose fouled off one, another, four in a row. Seidman scowled. He tried a curve ball and it was high and outside.

With the count full, Jose backed out of the box, wiped his hands, picked up some dirt, rubbed it, took a firm, choked grip on the big bat. He stepped in again, hesitated, looked over at Junior.

Junior said, "*Woof!*"

Seidman took his time. He wound up, unwound, went to the sidearm. He aimed the ball.

It was too close.

"Takeyerbase!" the umpire intoned, pronouncing it as one word.

Junior stood on his hind legs and pawed at the South Hollywood bench. Up in the stands, Lion came to his full, impressive height and purred like a smooth-running Rolls-Royce.

Sampson glanced at Coach Johnson, took a sign and went to the plate. Seidman tugged at his cap, kicked the rubber, knocked dirt from a spike and inhaled.

On the first pitch, Sampson put down a bunt on the first-base marking. Seidman threw him out while Jose danced down to second.

Hatfield took the same sign, nodded. He also bunted the first ball. It rolled foul and Jose had to go back to the bag. Hatfield pop-fouled the second throw with the same result.

Seidman heaved a sigh, squinted at Jose and seemed to regain confidence as he threw a breaking ball. Hatfield swung at it. He was overeager. He struck out.

Jack Pilgrim went to Junior and looked into his large brown eyes. Junior growled and licked the extended hand. Jack grinned at the Coach and went to the bat rack and picked up his favorite weapon.

Down at second base, Jose did not take a big lead. He waited until Seidman was on the rubber. Then he began walking off the bag, slowly but surely edging toward third.

Out beyond center field, in the station wagon, Syd Grimm said, "He's goin' too far off."

"He's off altogether," said Otto indifferently. "Let's head for the beach."

"No, I got to see this," Grover said. "He's goin' to be caught."

"Sure, he is," said Sandy. "They got him!"

But Seidman had committed himself. He must now throw the ball or be guilty of a balk. Upset by Jose's daring, he simply chucked it as hard as he could, right over the plate.

Jack wasn't swinging for the fence this time. He met the

ball fair and sound and smacked it into right field. Jose, with his big head start, turned third and flew like a swallow down the line for the platter. Jack held up at first. There was no throw. Ober knew when he was beaten. He held the ball and kept Jack from advancing.

Seidman sighed. But he showed his courage, then. He made Harry Keel pop out to the catcher to end the frame.

Now it was six to five and Tod Hunter had to pitch to the South Hollywoods. The stout boy was bathed in perspiration when he took off his jacket. He went over and laid a hand on Junior's big skull and said, "Wish me luck, pal."

The crowd was tense. The power hitters had been helpless before Tod's delivery, but there was a feeling that it couldn't last forever. Calvin, Mount and Kelly were due in order and these were stalwart athletes. Tod fiddled around, staring at the leadoff man.

Calvin stared right back. He waggled a big stick that seemed loaded with dynamite. Tod toed the rubber, threw a fast ball, low and inside.

Calvin lashed at it. The horsehide went slightly to Tod's right, heading for a sure hit to center field. Jose took off with the sound of bat on ball. He hurled himself at the ball. It stuck in his glove.

He spun and threw in the same motion. Harry Keel stretched a mile to meet it. The umpire, bent and intent, threw up a thumb.

"Yerout!"

Tod plucked a blade of grass, walking toward Jose. "Between you and your dog, *amigo*, I live."

Jose replied. "Nice going, *amigo*. Throw it at 'em."

But Tod was tiring. The extra pounds were taking their toll. He slipped a bit and hung one for Mount. The left fielder of the Suns slapped it into right field for a clean single.

It was the first hit off Tod and the South Hollywood bench came up as one man, screaming for Kelly to hit it out of the park. The Green Sox fans fell silent until Mr. Vale again urged them to get to work.

Jose ran in as Fred Barker came out to talk with the pitcher. "Let 'em hit it," he urged.

"That's right," said Fred. "You've got men behind you, fat boy. Keep it low and let 'em hit it."

Tod said, "They hit it real good off poor Birkie."

"He didn't keep it low," said Barker, and went back to squat behind the plate.

Jose returned to his position. He shaded Kelly, a left-handed hitter, a bit toward second base. Nick Farmer followed, giving the third-base line to the Sun player. Kelly could not refrain from taking a longing glance at the wide-open space.

Tod quickly fed him a fast ball on his wrists, so that he could not push it. Kelly, a very quick boy, came around and hit the ball on the nose.

Jose flashed to his right. He reached for the bounce, nailed it, threw for second without looking.

Aki came in, grabbed the ball, jumped away from Mount's slide and slammed across the diamond. Harry Keel extended his fishnet mitt.

"Yerout!" chanted the umpire and the double play was

completed to end the ball game. Jose came racing to grab Tod Hunter and pound his back as they all ran for the clubhouse to celebrate.

The bench overturned in the excitement. Junior found himself free as the afternoon air. He ambled along, dragging his chain, anxious to join the party.

Lion seemed satisfied with the result of the contest. He daintily jumped down the stands, row by row.

They suddenly confronted one another, the big cat and the gigantic dog. People saw them and scattered. Jose remembered and came racing back. Coach Johnson, blaming himself, was close behind.

Junior lowered his head. Lion crouched, whiskers curving, trembling in the breeze. The eyes of the dog and cat met and locked.

Jose's heart was in his throat. Jack Pilgrim was hurtling through the crowd, passing Johnson.

Then Junior said, *"Woof?"*

The big cat nestled down. *"Meow?"*

The would-be peacemakers skidded to a halt. The two animals put their heads together. Junior, true to form, stuck out his long tongue in an attempting to lick Lion's head. The cat got up, gurgled in his throat and walked toward the bicycle rack. The dog started to follow, as though he had been invited.

Jose grabbed the leash and said, "That is enough for today, no? You are a lucky dog, I think."

It was no task to get the Saint Bernard to the dressing rooms. Junior liked everybody and everything, but he knew where he had the most friends—among his ball-players. They made a wonderful fuss over him.

But not as much fuss as they made over Tod Hunter and Jose.

Tod said, "For a fat pitcher and a no-hit shortstop, we did all right out there, at that."

Still, Jose thought, even as they praised him, it had largely been a matter of pat ball hitting and good luck—at least he thought it was luck.

Coach Johnson and Jack Pilgrim thought differently. They thought it was courage and determination and did not hesitate to say so.

In the station wagon, which was heading for the beach, Otto was saying, "If they'd played him right, they woulda got him. He didn't have a right to score."

Syd did not join in the ensuing discussion. He was silently wondering if he could have done as well as the scorned Jose Cansino.

9

It was a strange season, Jack Pilgrim thought, as he paused to feed Lion early on a Friday morning, many weeks after the South Hollywood game.

"You can twitch your ears and slurp up food and act like a king," he said. "You can believe it, but I don't. Sure, we won ten games in a row. And Woodland High's not the best team in the conference. And we should beat them easy in tomorrow's game. But how did we do it?"

His own batting average was good, .345. But no one else was hitting very well. Aki was down to a miserable .210 and even Freddy Barker was only at .250. The pitching for the opposition had been terrific, Jack conceded.

Jose Cansino was at .256, which was good for a hot-fielding shortstop. But Jose's value was far in excess of his average. He was always on base when needed. There had been one-sided games in which Jose could not buy his way to first base. It was in the tight ones, the near-losses, that he popped up on first, to be driven around by Jack or Harry Keel or Joe Sampson.

"It's weird, but we would be noplace without that little shortstop," Jack went on, addressing his favorite audience. "And the funny part of it is, he won't recognize it. He thinks he is not playing well enough because he makes errors. Golly, he gets his hands on grounders that nobody else could come close to; why shouldn't he blow a few?"

Aki Matsuo had come up behind him in his usual quiet way. "You are right, Jack. Excuse me, I could not help overhearing."

"The kid works too hard. He gets A grades, he stays out there and practices night after night." This was not the first time Jack and Aki had conferred alone in the time before the student body gathered for the day.

"He will not work today," Aki said, frowning. "I stopped by his house. He is confined with a fever."

"No!"

"His mother says it is not serious, just a slight fever. Probably the 'virus X' which is going around."

"But how about tomorrow?"

"I would not count upon him," replied Aki. "It should be an easy game and Jay is improving."

"Young Byron's too green," Jack thought aloud. "He'll be all right two years from now."

"We had better see the coach," suggested Aki.

"Yes. Of all the guys on the team—" Jack broke off, unwilling to hurt Aki, knowing of the second baseman's anguish about his batting average.

"Don't be afraid to say it," Aki told him softly. "I too

have respect for Jose. He is," he hesitated, grinned widely and went on, "*muy caballero.*"

"Hey, you're a linguist!"

I study Spanish in Mr. Linguisi's class." They were walking toward the gym entry now. Lion was staring after them, aware that something was wrong, somewhat miffed at being ignored. After a moment, he ambled into the school by another entrance and began his daily parade of the halls. When the students came in, he greeted them quite as though he was well acquainted with each and every individual. And who was to say that he was not?

There was a slight problem gnawing at Lion's ego. For years he had not permitted any other animal to come near Studio City High School except on a fleeting visit. Now he had no way of doing anything about the enormous dog who appeared every Saturday to raucous cheers from everyone. It was not that Lion was jealous. After all, Saturday was not a regular school day. All the rest of the week it was Lion's own kingdom—he jolly well saw to that. And when were all the girls and boys in the corridors, in the classrooms, in the assembly hall? Right—during Lion's regime.

Why, even the teachers paused to speak with him—all excepting Miss Dorothy Jayson. She was afraid of cats. She once fainted at sight of a kitten brought in by a girl who thought Lion would like to play with it. There was something wrong with Miss Jayson.

There was something wrong with any girl who thought Lion would waste time playing with a baby cat, also, but at least the girl had meant well. Miss Jayson was a nervous kind of woman, and Lion was glad to stay out of her path. He preferred Mr. Vale's secretary, who brought him little tidbits when she thought about it. And of course there was no one like Jack Pilgrim, who thought about feeding his cat friend every morning, including Saturday, now the day of the dog.

Lion hoisted his tail and bowed to the janitor and paraded toward the Principal's office, while down in the gym there was worriment.

Coach Johnson was saying to the two boys, "We can make it. I talked to Mrs. Cansino and she doesn't think Jose is seriously ill. Mainly, he's fretting about the game tomorrow. Maybe you should go by and speak with him after school—reassure him."

"We'll do that," Jack promised. He did not look very happy.

Aki said, "Jay is a fine prospect, sir. He can work into the job this afternoon, can't he?"

"I'm afraid to tell him," confessed the Coach. "That kid blushes and stammers when you look at him."

"He's a nice fella, though," Jack insisted.

"Very nice," Aki added.

They were all wondering the same thing: could the nice green kid hold up for one game, possibly more, if Jose came down with the flu or something that would keep him out of the crucial contest with the Bellingham Bells?

The Bells had sailed through the season without further mishap. They were in second place, since Studio City had not lost a game.

Coach Johnson had used his pitchers wisely to get thus

far undefeated. Tod Hunter had gone against the big but slower hitters. Al Birkie had been unbeatable against the smarter clubs. It was necessary to choose who would pitch against the Woodland Woodys tomorrow, whether to give Birkie a workout he might need or to save him from possible accident by keeping him out altogether.

He said aloud, "Maybe we'll start with Al tomorrow, then use Tod about the sixth inning. Then they'll both have some exercise and be ready for Bellingham."

Jack declared, "That sounds good, Coach. We'll be all right tomorrow. I'm really worried about Jose and how he feels. He's my *amigo*, you know."

"Mine, too," said Aki.

"He's a remarkable boy," agreed Johnson. "By the way, have you noticed that Syd Grimm's dropout friends are around again?"

"I thought they had jobs?"

"They were box boys in a supermart, I found. The school authorities have had their eyes on them since the incidents of the false alarms. Syd was doing pretty good classwork while they weren't around. Now he's with them again, every afternoon."

"Syd doesn't have any other friends," Aki remarked. "It can be lonely."

Aki would know about loneliness, the other two realized. Until he had been unceremoniously thrust into a responsible position on the ball team and had made good, very few of the students had offered him companionship.

"There's nothing we can do about Syd," said Jack. "He's

sore at all of us. He never stopped making remarks about Jose."

"And me," added Aki. "It is necessary to ignore him. He can be very loud and very cruel."

"Continue to ignore him," Johnson cautioned them. "I don't want you boys in any trouble."

"No trouble, Coach," they promised him.

It was time to go to their home rooms. The pair parted in the hallway, each with his own thoughts about Jose and tomorrow's game.

Jack Pilgrim was at his locker an hour later that morning. As he reached for a notebook, he disturbed his reserve outfielder's glove. Beneath it was the scrap of cloth from someone's trousers which he had found all those weeks ago at the scene of the crime....

Just then, the fire alarm went off.

Jack put the cloth in his pocket. Then he went on a run up the stairs and in the direction of the box which had been used in the previous fakes.

He was correct. It was the same fire box which had been attacked.

He whirled around, ignoring the clamor of the student body as the drill took place. It had occurred to him that there must be a reason why this particular box should be used each time. He had been on the scene before but had seen no one. He had only heard the slap of flat feet.

He walked around the turn in the corridor, which was the place from whence he had heard those sounds echoing. Where had the fleeing culprits escaped to so swiftly?

There was a snarling growl. He saw Lion crouched for

attack in the middle of the hallway—yet there was no one in sight. The tall figure of Mr. Vale came into view.

"That you, Pilgrim? Why aren't you taking part in the drill?"

"Because it's another false alarm, sir." Jack indicated the broken glass of the box.

"And how did you know that, Pilgrim?"

Jack felt himself flushing like Jay Byron. "Because I . . . well, I just happened to have my hand on . . . Well, sir, I'm afraid I haven't exactly been honest about this."

"You what? *You*, Pilgrim?" Mr. Vale was shocked to the core.

"Well, you see I found this piece of cloth." Jack blinked, paused. "Oh, sir, you don't think I did it?"

Mr. Vale took the bit of material from Jack's hand. "You had me worried for a minute. What about this, now?"

"I heard footsteps, I told about that. Only . . . well, an athlete hears certain things different, I guess. The guys running were flat-footed. But that sounds silly, and I didn't want to . . . Well, it sounds silly," he ended weakly.

"I don't agree. Flat-footed, eh? And this seems to be a piece of cloth torn out of a pair of trousers." Vale looked up and down the corridor. "What's Lion doing there?"

Lion was making deep, growling sounds in his throat. His tail was swishing as though he meant to sweep up the entire third floor. His ruff stood straight out and seemed to emit electricity.

"*Grrrrowl*," insisted the cat.

Jack's gaze went around and about, until, suddenly, it fastened on a door opposite Lion's position. It was marked plainly, "Maintenance." The space inside was for the purpose of storing booms and other cleaning apparatus. There was one or two of these closets on each floor. They were supposed to be locked at all times, to prevent fun-loving students from strewing the contents inside through the halls of learning.

Mr. Vale had the same idea at the same time. "That cat! Smartest creature in school."

"I think it was Lion who tore loose that swatch of cloth," said Jack. "He's awful tough sometimes."

"All the time," corrected Mr. Vale. "Well, are you ready?"

"Yes, sir. I . . . I guess so."

"We need only trap one." Mr. Vale was whispering. "He'll talk, if we keep a grip on him."

"Yes, sir." Would it be Syd Grimm? Jack hoped it would not be. He and Syd had been good friends, once upon a time.

"You open the door," said the Principal. "I'll catch hold of the first one out."

"Better still, sir, you open the door. I play football, remember?"

"You do as I say," ordered Mr. Vale. He removed his horn-rimmed spectacles, jammed them in his breast pocket. "This is my job."

Jack had to obey. He crept close to the door. Estimating the distance to the knob, he set himself. He had to jerk the door toward him. Meanwhile, he noticed that Mr. Vale had slipped to the other side of the portal.

Lion meowed approval and did not give an inch, block-ing the middle of the hallway. If it had been any other cat, Jack would have felt it incumbent upon him to chase him away. Lion, he felt, could cope with any situation.

He took a deep breath, reached out and turned the knob silently, then slammed open the door. There was the sound of flight and sudden contact, then scuffling before Jack could get from behind the door. Lion let out a howl.

Mr. Vale was hurled to the other side of the hall. Three figures were flying, flat-footed. Jack took off after them.

Then one of them went down and there was a noise like lions let loose. This slowed the parade. Jack came up behind the fleeing boys as another of them fell and began to howl, "It's scratchin' my eyes out!"

Mr. Vale was gamely coming on. Jack got a hold on the shoulder of Grover and spun him to his feet.

Mr. Vale descended upon Sandy, picked him up and jammed him against the wall, while Lion hovered, spitting. Otto was gone with the wind and Grover was all for joining him.

Jack tried hard to merely hold the fighting dropout. He was taking a few punches in the process.

He heard Mr. Vale's voice behind him call sharply, "Hit him, Jack!"

Grover sunk a hard right hand to the body, then tried to bring up a knee. Jack stepped away, letting go his hold on the scared, fighting intruder. Grover almost fell down, but recovered to swing a haymaker at Jack's head.

Jack reluctantly shifted, dropping back his right foot, levering a left hook which started from the hip. His fist connected with Grover's jaw.

Grover fell down and lay still. Lion walked over and sat

deliberately upon his chest, blinking and purring, thoroughly satisfied.

"Two out of three, that's pretty good," said Mr. Vale.

"You got no cause to do this to us," cried Sandy. "You're violatin' our constitution rights."

"That's what they all say, all the criminals, old and young," said Mr. Vale, who was suffering slightly from the first charge, which had roughly bowled him aside. "Shall we go down to my office?"

The students were beginning to file back into the school. Sandy yelled, "I ain't goin' anyplace," and wrenched away and began to run.

Since Grover at this moment began bucking a bit, Jack was forced to put an armlock on him and help him, swaying, to his feet. Sandy got all the way to the end of the hall, with Mr. Vale in hot pursuit.

Aki Matsuo's class was coming into view. The small Japanese boy saw the Principal chasing someone and acted without thought. He stepped out of line.

Sandy lowered his head and extended a football stiff-arm. It seemed as though the little second baseman would be impaled, destroyed.

Aki dipped a shoulder, moved his feet and caught hold of Sandy's outstretched wrist. He made another maneuver, too quick to follow.

Sandy described a pretty parabola, making a circle of his body, with flying arms and legs. He smacked against the wall, sank to the floor and moaned, "Everyone's against me!" Then he was quite still.

Mr. Vale adjusted his clothing and said, "Er, Matsuo,

would you kindly escort that young individual down to my office?"

"Yes, sir," said Aki obediently, as Jack arrived with Grover in tow. He had recognized the prisoners by now and had an idea of what was happening. He bowed to Jack, winking, and added, "After you, *amigo*."

"I want my father!" Grover was weeping, holding his face with both hands. "You broke my jaw."

Sandy chorused, "That dirty Jap used judo on me. My father'll take care of him."

The teachers had a bit of trouble getting the other students into their classrooms as Jack and Aki marched their captives to the stairway. No one, however, missed the sight of Lion following triumphantly behind, his head and tail erect, stiff as a ramrod.

Jack Pilgrim and Aki Matsuo sat in Jose Cansino's bedroom and told him the story.

"There was old Syd Grimm in the fire drill, minding his own business," Jack was saying. "I don't think he even knew about the false alarm. He might have guessed his pals were guilty, but he didn't know about it, wasn't in on it."

Jose reached for a glass of water at his bedside. He looked pale and somehow very small in his pajamas. "That is very good. I did not like to think Syd would be so foolish."

Aki said, "It was remarkable the way Sandy and Grover squealed—like piglets under a fence."

"Amazing," agreed Jack. "They hollered cop, then they hollered for Mama and Papa. Then, when Mr. Vale and the truant officer and the policemen showed up, they began to cry and said Otto put them up to it. Some tough guys they turned out to be!"

Aki continued, "And then, Jose, they began to blame everything upon us. You and me, we are foreigners who have all the best of it, while they have nothing."

Jack was embarrassed. "You guys know the rest of the school thinks differently. You know that."

There was a split second of silence, then Jose replied, "You were always good to me, *amigo*. You were my friend."

"And mine," agreed Aki. "And furthermore, why should we not earn our way? It seems to me all the kids have to find out who they are, then show their colors."

"*Sí, sí!*" cried Jose. "I agree with that. Tomorrow little Jay Byron will have to earn his place. It is the same with all."

"Leaving out the name-calling," Jack interposed.

Junior, who had scarcely left the sickroom since Jose was put to bed, thumped his tail on the floor. He seemed fully aware of the circumstances. He had greeted Jack and Aki with affection but with some reserve, not quite up to his usual effusions. His mournful eyes remained constantly upon the boy in the bed.

Mama Cansino, bright, bustling, amazingly young and pretty, came in with a platter of cookies and a pitcher of lemonade and an antibiotic pill for Jose. The boys got to their feet and she smiled at them and said, "Five minutes, please? He must be quiet, then. He has the television, and he has Junior, no? Does Junior carry the germs, do you think?"

"Oh, no, Mrs. Cansino," Aki assured her. "Not human germs."

They all laughed and Mrs. Cansino went back to her household chores and Jose made a face and took his pill. The visitors munched cookies and drank the cold lemonade.

Jack said, "Well, it's an easy game tomorrow, anyway. You just have to get well and get your strength back for the Bells next Saturday."

"I am weaker than tissue paper," fretted Jose. "This virus X, the doctors do not know what it is, so they use algebra. X! I feel like an ex-shortstop."

"You'll be all right. You've got over a week to recover," said Aki.

Jose asked suddenly, "What will happen to those three who were caught?"

"Why, I don't really know," answered Jack, surprised. "You're not worrying about them, are you?"

"They're just kids—like us." Jose was uncomfortable, but stubborn. "It would be bad if they were sent away, would it not, *amigo?*"

The trio were solemnly silent, considering the shadowy horror of being "sent away" to the reform school, which was known under a different name but no less frightening.

"They are, after all, not criminals," Aki added.

"They have nothing to do with their time. They cannot get decent jobs," Jose pointed out. "They hang around school all the time, when they are free to do so. Why do they come back to the school grounds?"

"Well, I guess they kind of miss it," suggested Jack.

"Dropouts, they have a problem. I read about it in the

newspaper," said Aki. "It is sad. They seek freedom and then they find they do not really want it."

"What's so tough about school?" asked Jack.

"To some of them, it must be very difficult," Aki observed. "To us, it is a privilege. I think this problem is too much for us, now."

"Too much for me," said Jack. It was time to leave. "I've got enough trouble keeping up in chemistry. Right now, those books are haunting me. Get well, *amigo*. We need you."

"Jay will do all right." Jose was sleepy, probably a result of the pills he was taking. "See you *mañana*—tomorrow, my good friends."

Junior accompanied the visitors to the door of the bedroom, but would not budge another step. Jack realized there was no use asking if the mascot would be with them on the morrow. It would be impossible to separate the big dog from his master and mentor.

When the pair were on Curzon Street, Aki asked, "Do you think he will be all right next week?"

"I've had that virus X," Jack responded. "It knocks you out for a couple of days, then goes away. You're weak for maybe two more days. He should be well enough to play against the Bells."

"That is good." Aki waved farewell and went on his way toward his home. Jack mounted his bike and rode off, his mind going to his chemistry experiment.

As he pedaled, he was aware that someone was following him in a car. He slowed down, glanced over his shoulder. He recognized the old station wagon owned by Syd

Grimm and steered up a driveway and onto the sidewalk, dismounted and prepared to defend himself.

Syd put on the brakes and pulled into the curb. He got out of the car and walked slowly to where Jack waited for him. There was obviously no fight in him.

"Hi, Jack," he muttered. "Wanted to talk to you."

"But not to Aki. Nor Jose," said Jack, grim-faced.

Immediately the other boy flared up. "Why should I talk to them?"

"You never thought about apologizing?"

"Apologizing?" Syd's neck began to swell. "Look, I just wanted to tell you I didn't have anything to do with setting off those false alarms. I think that was a stupid and childish thing to do. That's all."

Jack shrugged and waited.

"Well, that's all I wanted to tell you."

"Okay. You told me."

Syd's voice became louder. "Those guys are friends of mine. I'm not about to let 'em down because they're in trouble, I'm telling you that right now."

"That's two things you told me, Syd."

"Nothing's going to happen to them, either. So they get a bawling-out. Maybe they get some kind of probation. It was just a kid trick."

"Some kids," Jack couldn't help observing. "Your pal Grover tried to beat up on me."

"He was only trying to get away. Anybody'd run in a spot like that."

"And I suppose I shouldn't have tried to stop him?"

"Well, it was kind of a finky thing to do. Let the Principal and the teachers handle that kind of thing."

"Oh, boy!" exclaimed Jack. "Whatever happened to you, Syd? We used to be friends. Now you're out there on cloud nine—or someplace. You don't even make sense." He forbore to mention that he had held back two small pieces of evidence because he was afraid they might implicate Syd.

"Well, anybody who acts like Otto and Grover and Sandy are some kind of kooks."

"I don't know about that. But I know Sandy and Grover squealed on Otto. They even told about a piece of cloth torn out of Otto's pants in the earlier false alarm stunt. You talk about finks?"

"They were on the spot. They were scared. Wouldn't you be?"

"Why, yes, I guess I would be. I've been scared plenty of times. But I wouldn't turn in false alarms in the first place, you see. Like you say, it's dumb and childish."

Syd was baffled, frustrated. "You just don't want to understand anything. You're like all the rest."

Jack heaved a deep sigh. "The truth is, I don't get it. You and your pals call names. You get fired from the baseball team. So then the whole world is wrong and you're right. What's with you, Syd?"

"I attend classes. I get my grades. It's nobody's business who I hang out with after school."

"Right," agreed Jack. "It's all your business. Then why bring it to me?"

"Because we did use to be friends," blurted Syd. "I don't want you gettin' any wrong ideas about me."

Jack stifled a sharp retort. He leaned on the handles of his bicycle and looked hard at Syd. It was growing late by his watch. Only because of daylight saving was the sun still alive in the pleasant, warm evening.

"All right, skip it, Syd," he said. "Been surfin' lately?"

"We were out Sunday for a while. It wasn't much good." But surfing reminded Syd of his three friends. He went on, "Well, that's about it, I guess. I'm not turning them down, remember."

Jack adjusted the pedals of his bike. "Like you said. Be seeing you around."

He rode off. As he turned the corner, heading toward home, he looked back. Syd was still standing on the sidewalk, lost in thought. It seemed impossible that this was the old buddy with whom he had done so many companionable things, had so much fun. It was sad to remember those times.

How had it all started?

With the name-calling, he knew. It just went against the grain to hear kids called "greaser" and "Jap-boy" and things like that. He wasn't being noble or anything. Most of the other kids detested it as much as he. The rest were plain ignorant. Joe Sampson had been a friend to Syd also, and he had walked away from that kind of talk.

Jack pumped up a slight grade. This was something over which he had no control, he decided. If Syd wanted to be friends, he shouldn't hang around with types like Otto and Sandy and Grover.

Jack's ribs still ached where Grover had connected during the battle in the hallway.

He remembered Lion perched proudly on Grover's

chest and had to chuckle to himself as he sped into the driveway of his home. It was Lion who had smelled out the hiding place of the miscreants. They had used the closet before, it had been learned, letting the hullabaloo die down while they crowded in there, laughing . . . then escaping at their leisure when everyone was busy in the classrooms. Otto had found a key which would work the lock of the broom closet. They were pretty clever about it, but old Lion wasn't fooled. The cat very nearly had grabbed them the first time, taking a piece of Otto's pants for a souvenir.

It was funny, all right, Jack thought, unstrapping his books from the carrier on the bike and heading for the house. Foiled by a cat!

11

The Studio City team rode a bus to Woodland, which was fifteen miles out the San Fernando Valley's Ventura Freeway. A parade of private automobiles followed, with banners of green and white flying and horns blowing. There were three motion picture stars and four radio announcers to greet the players, since Woodland was the home of many of these professional people.

There was also a brass band, playing the Woodland High song and *Tiger Rag, The Saints Come Marching In,* and other rousing numbers. The musicians were professionals from the television, radio and motion picture business. It was a bit overwhelming, like playing in the big leagues, Jack Pilgrim thought, as he descended from the bus and faced the crowd.

There was a line of short-skirted girls with white jerseys bearing a huge "W" of bright orange. They carried pompons and were all exceptionally pretty. Most of them were the daughters of actors and actresses, and they had an air of sophistication lacking in the young people of other Valley high schools.

One of them cried out, "Oh, look at the cute one!"

"*Whee!* He's just way out there!"

"Can I have him for my very own?"

Jack craned to see who was getting this special attention. He saw Jay Byron stuck to the steps of the bus as though someone had poured glue around the soles of his shoes. The young boy's face was a crimson shade which threatened the brilliance of the California sun. He was shaking like a palmetto in a sea breeze, but there was no cool zephyr for Jay; he was hot with utter embarrassment.

Jack plunged back through the crowd to the substitute shortstop's side. He grabbed Jay's arm and yanked him to earth, then hustled him in the wake of the others as they carried their bags to the dressing room of the high-school gymnasium.

"Pay no attention to them. They're just trying to get your goat," he warned Jay.

"They . . . they got it," confessed the younger boy. "I . . . I wasn't ready for anything like that."

"Just concentrate on playing ball," begged Jack. "This is a wild bunch of kids, but they don't mean any harm. Last year we played in Studio City and they brought a big band, remember? And acrobats to lead cheers, a lot of stuff like that. We beat 'em 8 to 0. They have fun, but they're not such great ballplayers."

"I know," said Jay. "It's just that I get so nervous."

"Well, cut it out," pleaded Jack. "It's the worst thing you can do. Just concentrate. Forget the people."

"I'll try." Jay looked as though he were about to weep.

Jack departed to seek Coach Johnson. If there had been another sub infielder, he would have suggested a change in the plan, but the Green Sox were weak on the bench that season, especially since the departure of Grimm and Cohen. He merely warned the coach that Jay was jittery.

"Well, it's his first start," said Johnson. "He'll settle down. He's a good boy."

Anything more would sound like carping, so Jack went to a corner and began dressing in the green and white spangles which he had worn so proudly for three years. His final season would soon be over and he wanted it to be a success. He wanted that championship for the school; it really meant a lot to him.

Coach Rabbit Marx, a tiny gnome of a man, old in the service of the school system, popped into the dressing room and shook hands with Chuck Johnson. Surveying the boys as they dressed, he chattered like a magpie.

"So this is the team that beat the Bells. A great crowd you got here, Chuck; great. Husky bunch of athletes. Sure will be rough on my poor little kids. Are you going to pitch your left-hander against us? No? Maybe? That's right, don't tip off anything." His eyes were darting about, merry and full of questions. "Oh, there's the cute one. I hear your regular shortstop is sick. Too bad, but you don't have to worry about us; Bellingham beat us to pieces. Say, he is cute, at that!"

Standing beside pink-cheeked Jay Byron, he affectionately tousled the boy's hair. "You'll be fine, fellow. Don't let those little gals get your nanny." He trotted toward the door, paused, turned and repeated, "Sure is cute. I can see what they mean." Then he was gone.

"He thinks he's Casey Stengel," Coach Johnson said. "Always with the jokes. Let's get organized here. Al, you're going to start, so go over the hitters with Barker. You others, trot out there and learn about the field. Let's get going!"

But Jack knew that the team was not settled down when after the preliminaries were over and the umpires had taken their places and called "Time!" Jay Byron was cowering at the bat rack. The pompon girls were leaping up and down and chirping, "He's cute! He's cute! He's cute!" and the stands were stomping their feet as though it were a last-inning rally with the home team a run behind. The brass band was tootling and the happy Hollywood people were cheering their sons.

In the box for Woodland was a tall, lean, freckled, red-haired boy named Galloway. Last year he had been just a fair performer and Marx hadn't used him much this season, but Jack always watched the warm-ups and he had an uneasy feeling that the opposing hurler might be about ready. He had seen this before, as with their own Tod Hunter. One day, the player was just ordinary, the next, he had blossomed into a formidable athlete. This could be the day for the easy-grinning Woodlander.

Coach Johnson was saying to Bryon, "This Galloway has a tendency to be wild. Wait him out. That's what you have to learn, Byron; look 'em over. Let the bad ones go by."

"Yes, sir," said Jay.

Jack doubted that the boy heard what the coach had said. His ears were throbbing with the cry, "He's cute! He's cute."

The band played *Seventy-six Trombones* as loudly as possible. Jay's knees were knocking together as he went to the plate.

Morgan, the husky catcher of the Woodys, said, "Here's the cute kid, Red. Feed it to him. The girls want to see him get a hit!"

Jay crouched, making as small a target as possible. Jack wondered if he could see the ball at all. This was a terrible initiation for a shy kid.

Galloway wound up and seemed to throw carelessly, a straight, hard pitch around the knees. Jay remembered what the Coach had told him, all right. He let it go by.

"Stuh—rike!" said the umpire, who was a thin man and right in the spirit of Woodland High, with a loud voice which made Jay jump in surprise.

Morgan returned the ball to the pitcher. He squatted, gave the sign, then said conversationally to Jay, "You got to take the bat off your shoulder to be a hitter, Cutie."

At that instant, Galloway threw another fast ball. It also got the corner of the plate for a strike.

Now Jay was wild with anger at himself, at the cheering section, at the catcher and at the ball and bat. When the redheaded hurler threw him a slow change-up, he swung with all his might. He went completely around in a circle, as if trying to corkscrew himself into the ground. Then he fell down.

"Cute! Cute! Cute!" the opposition were yelling.

Jay got up, dusted himself off. He walked slowly and grimly to the bat rack and carefully replaced his stick. He went to the bench, yanked down his cap and sat hunched and blank-faced.

Sampson went to bat. Galloway grinned at him, resumed his easy, natural pitching. Sampson swung twice, missed both apparently easy tosses. His third attempt was a pop fly to Downey, the Woodland elongated first-sacker.

Hatfield went up. As Sampson walked past him, Jack asked, "What's he got on the ball, anyway?"

"Nothin'," replied the left fielder. "Not a single, gol-durned thing."

Hatfield hit a weak grounder to short, which was gobbled up by Tully and thrown to first for easy out.

Jack replaced his bat and remarked, "He's doing all right out there with nothin' on the ball."

As he went to pick up his glove, he automatically looked for Junior. It was a moment before he realized that the Saint Bernard was at home with his master. It didn't seem right.

Nothing seemed right. It was a lovely, clear, sunny day, but there was something amiss. Was it the fact that they missed Jose and Junior? It wasn't sensible for one man—and one dog—to make all that difference, Jack argued to himself. He went to center field and waited for Birkie to subdue the casual, easy-going Woodlanders.

Birkie was his usual adept self. He had the best curve

ball in high-school ranks, and he always could control his pitches. He went to work on Hall, a lanky left fielder who led off for the Woodys. He quickly got two strikes on his man.

Then Hall brought his bat around in a half swing, as though merely protecting the plate. The ball skidded off the wood and down between third and short.

It was Jay's ball, but Nick Farmer became overprotective and tried to make the play. He bobbled the ball. Jay picked it up and threw too hard and too quick, always the sign of an inexperienced player.

The ball sailed over Harry Keel's upthrust glove. Hall went to second.

Jack murmured, "Wow, two errors on one play!"

The next hitter was Downey, the first baseman. He stood up there as though he were put together in sections, like a mechanical toy. Birkie threw him a fast curve.

Downey snapped his swing. He got ahead of the ball hitting from the port side of the plate. He slammed it into left field for a single.

Hall scored.

Porter, a stocky lad, Woodland's right fielder, was next. Birkie was walking around the mound talking to himself. The colorful cheer leaders and gay fans of Woodland were whooping it up. Jack thumped a fist into his glove.

In the next instant, he was running to his left. Porter had blooped one into no man's land. It fell safely and Jack had to one-hand it to make the throw.

Jay should have made the cutoff to hold the runners. Instead, he was out of position and the ball skipped past

Nick Farmer, and everyone advanced. That put Downey on third and Porter on first, with one run in. Yet no one had hit a decent knock off Birkie.

The pitcher was a cool one, however. He motioned that everything was all right and went to work on the best Woodland slugger, Bernstein, a husky second baseman. Birkie worked to the full count, then Einstein hit the curve ball.

Jack, already playing deep, retreated. He caught the ball in throwing position. He knew Downey would score from third after the catch. He leaned and threw off Porter at third.

Jay Byron cut off the throw. The run came in and Porter easily made third.

Now it was Foster, the Woodland center fielder. Again Birkie got two strikes on him and again the batter hit a long fly to center. All Jack could do was run and jump and make a difficult catch.

Porter scored after the catch.

Birkie struck out the third baseman, Hanson, and went off the field shaking his head. The Woodland High team had three runs on two dinky, lucky hits.

Jack took his bat, again looked for Junior, frowned, went to the plate. Coach Johnson was explaining the cut-off to Jay Byron, but he might as well save his breath, Jack thought. The kid was simply stampeded. They were still howling "Cute!" at him and he was the kind of boy who would rather fight than be the center of attention. In time, he would outgrow this, but right now he was a sure shot to blush at the drop of a pompon.

Galloway regarded Jack as though he were a specimen beneath a microscope in a science class. Morgan said, "Just another yokel from the sticks, Red. Let's get him."

Jack did not move a muscle. He held the bat poised over his left shoulder, high in the air. He had estimated that Galloway was taking speed off his pitches and shrewdly finding spots which were difficult for the batter to cover. The first one was a whistling low pitch. Jack took it for a strike.

A moment later, Morgan tried the same old stunt, saying, "You got to take the bat off your shoulder, son," as Galloway lunged in with a sneak throw.

Jack was paying no attention at all to Morgan. He was looking for a ball to hit. . . .

He swung with everything he had. He felt the wood meet the leather and squinted after the flying baseball as he started for first. After a fast start, he slowed down. No outfielder in the high-school conference was going to get close to that one. It was out of sight and gone forever. At first base, Jack slowed down and faced the Woody cheerleaders.

"I'm the cute one," he told them. "Wave your little pompons at me."

They laughed and yelled good-naturedly as he paraded around the bases. They were wonderful sports, he realized. They were out to have fun, and if poor Jay couldn't take it, so much the better for them.

He went to the bench and told this to the shortstop, but young Byron seemed in a daze.

"I don't know, seems like everything is wrong. Coach

bawled me out for messin' up the cutoff. I never did get to practice it."

"All right, forget it," advised Jack. "Just stick in there and do the best you can."

"I'll try, honest I will."

"You'll be fine, if you can close your ears and pay attention."

"They make so much noise," Jay said, scowling. "I hate brass bands."

Aki Matsuo suddenly appeared, knelt between young Byron and Jack. He said, "Look, Jay, I was worse than you. Remember the first game? I was so scared I couldn't talk. Then I got mad."

"Mad?"

"Angry. At myself. It does a lot of good."

Jay was thoughtful. "I guess I am mad at me. I guess that's the main trouble."

"So get mad at them, too," Jack suggested. "What right have they got to pick on you?"

"That's it," agreed Aki. "What right?"

Jay glared belligerently over at the cheer leaders. "Yeah! Girls! They're a pain!"

Jack winked at Aki, who nodded. Jay would be all right.

On the mound, Galloway was hurling steadily. Seemingly without effort he got Keel to ground out, Farmer to fly out and Matsuo to hit a come-backer to the box where the redheaded pitcher easily threw him out.

Birkie, with the score three to one against him, was equally methodical. He struck out Tully, Morgan and with great satisfaction, Galloway.

Barker led off the third and popped out. Birkie stood in there and looked helplessly at three strikes. Now Jay Byron went to the plate for the second time.

The crowd began to chant, "He's cute! He's cute! He's cute!"

Galloway smiled and threw a fast curve ball which seemed about to plunk Jay in the ribs. The idea was to make the green boy jump away from a called strike.

Jay stuck in there. He brought the bat around as he had been taught, pulling for left field. There was a satisfying, smacking sound. Jay took his short, twinkling legs down to first in a breeze. He made the turn like a pro, bluffed toward second.

Out in right field, Porter fell for this move. He threw in great haste and the ball went wildly past the shortstop covering second. Jay kept right on and slid into the keystone sack in a cloud of dust.

Now the cheering became universal, the tone changing, "You're cute! You're cute! You're cute!"

Brushing dirt from his pants, Jay was bewildered for a moment. Then he realized the dancing cheer leaders were happy for him, that the happy-go-lucky Woodland fans had taken a fancy to him, win, lose or draw. He broke into a wide grin. He touched his cap in the traditional acknowledgment of the ballplayer from time immemorial.

In those brief seconds Jay Byron had truly become a ballplayer. Never again would he blush at the sound of his name, never would he be awed by the opposition, never again forget the mechanics of the game through nervousness. The odd adherents of Woodland High had helped make a man of him.

Galloway of Woodland did not join in the applause. He was a pitcher who begrudged every hit against him. He checked Jay's lead, eyes narrowed. He was no longer quite so casual pitching to Sampson. He worked the corners for a two and two count. He came in with the curve and Sampson missed it by a foot for the third strike.

Jay was stranded and Woodland still led in the game, 3 to 1.

As they ran onto the field, Aki said to Jay, "You see? Getting mad counted for you."

"Mad and scared," confessed the sub shortstop. "And thanks a lot, Aki."

"Thanks for nothing. You'll be all right."

And he was, and so was Aki. The innings rolled along, however, with no change in the score. Birkie continued to do his best. Galloway was perfect. Three up, three down, and even the Woodland rooters were becoming bored with the proceedings.

Beginning the ninth, Chuck Johnson sent in a pinch hitter for Birkie, which proved nothing, since Galloway got him to loft one to left. Jay manfully smacked one on the nose. Galloway leaped high and snared it.

"Can't that redhead do anything wrong?" demanded Coach Johnson. "Come on, Sampson, get a life!"

Sampson, with a good eye, again worked the count even, fouled one, let another ball go by. Galloway gamely tried his curve. It missed the corner and Sampson was on and the Green Sox bench began to clamor for victory.

Aki prayed, "Just a long one, over the fence and we'll beat them in the tenth."

Galloway was, indeed, having a bit of trouble with his control. He tried aiming the ball to Hatfield . . . and gave up another walk.

So two were on and Jack Pilgrim was at bat. A couple of runs to tie, a homer to go ahead. The noise was terrific. Jay and Aki were pounding each other, fully believing that their captain could do it again.

Galloway's jaw muscles were tight beneath the freckles. He pulled at his cap. He plucked at the resin bag. He walked around the mound, kicking at turf. He waved the Coach back as that worthy started onto the field. He rubbed a new ball and got back to position and bowed his neck.

He threw. Jack blinked as the ball zipped past him for a called strike.

Galloway checked the runner. He came to stretch position, a well-trained, cool young man. Jack set himself for the fast ball, ready to pounce.

The change-up came floating like a big toy balloon. Instantly Jack knew he should not hit at it. Just as quickly he realized he had committed himself, that he had to go through.

He was far out ahead of the pitch. He tried to push it into left field.

He popped it straight in the air. Galloway, as was fitting and proper, waved off his infielders and made the catch himself. The ball game was over.

Jack ran onto the field. He shook hands with the Woodland pitcher and said, "You were great. You sure deserved to win."

"A little lucky in the first inning," said Galloway graciously. "Your guy pitches up a pretty big storm himself. Hope you beat the Bells."

The Green Sox filed into the dressing room. Cheer leaders were still insisting Jay was cute. He felt rotten as Aki tried to cheer him. The Coach came to them.

"Jay, you did a wonderful job. From the first inning on you were the perfect shortstop. Aki will agree, you did all that could be asked of you."

"He was fine," said Aki. "Jose will be proud of you, Jay."

"Everybody get dressed," ordered Coach Johnson. "Stop feeling sorry for yourself. What team wins every game? It's a tie for the Conference and we have to get ready to beat the Bells."

Jay tried to smile. But he was not the only solemn Studio City player on the quiet bus ride home.

12

By Tuesday, Junior was slightly perplexed. It had been worrisome, with Jose in bed and unable to play. Missing the excitement of the baseball game was sad. But now Jose was off to that school again every day and Junior was left to his own devices, while the atmosphere had been gloomy ever since Jack Pilgrim had arrived Saturday with the bad news about their team's defeat.

The yard seemed altogether too small. Junior roamed up and he roamed down and then he flopped beneath his favorite bush and closed his eyes. It was just too much. He liked things simple and clear-cut. Happiness, that's what he craved, and people who were kind to him and allowed him to play with them.

He envied that big cat over at the school. Now there was a fellow being who had it all to himself—free to roam, to mingle with the boys and girls, to do anything he pleased. Maybe there were advantages in being a cat. But dogs belonged to people, while cats owned people. There was a great difference. It was bettter to be a Saint Bernard.

Lion, sitting in his favorite spot, high in the stands, at the practice field of Studio City High School, did not appear to agree. He had nothing against Junior, who was a friend of his friends; in fact, he had a slightly warm feeling toward the big dog, whom he sensed was not a threat to anybody.

Things were going so well down among the boys. Lion was a veteran of eight years of Green Sox baseball. He knew a lot about the players and the way they felt and how they were doing. Jack Pilgrim talked to him every morning and sometimes at night, too. He had done this very seriously during the past week.

The Cansino boy was back, but he was not allowed to work with the infield. He could only toss a ball back and forth and run slowly, trying to get back his strength. Lion knew Jose. He was the owner of the big dog and he also consulted with Jack and with the other small one, Aki Matsuo.

The Studio City players were worried because the shock of being beaten by Woodland High had not worn off. After all, if a sixth-place team can beat you, what chance have you against Bellingham? They were lucky to have beaten the Bells the first time. And with Jose not at his best, how could they be confident of winning the title in the playoff game this coming Saturday?

Oh, Lion had sensed it all in the tone of the morning talks. Jack kept telling everyone that they could win, that all they had to do was play their regular game of ball. But the others thought they needed all kinds of breaks in order to have a chance. Jack didn't believe in luck to win. He believed in solid baseball. When someone said maybe they had lost to the Woodys because that dog wasn't there, Jack had laughed at him.

The dog? That was pretty ridiculous. If they wanted an animal along, why hadn't they taken Lion?

As for the cat, he did not like automobiles, to tell the truth. He would rather stay right in the school grounds, where he belonged and was the ruler of all that moved. Only a dog would let himself be chained to the bench and show off for the multitude. That wasn't a cat trick. Lion would have fought, tooth and claw, anyone who tried to chain him up, even Jack . . . but then Jack would know better than to do such a thing.

Lion stretched, extended his front paws, sunk his curved talons into the wood, testing it for strength. There was a satisfying ripping sound. He walked slowly down the steps . . . forepaws, hindpaws, all with the huge dignity. He decided he would mingle a little and listen to the tone of their voices as they talked over the team's chances to beat Bellingham.

Jose was telling Jack Pilgrim, "I feel better, yes. In another day or two, the doctor will allow me to work as I should, no?"

"I hope so. Jay's improving every minute, now that he's got confidence. But he hasn't got your speed and savvy. And—well, we need you."

"I think Jay would do all right. I want to play, that is the thing. I have the desire to play against the Bells."

"You'll be in there," Jack promised. "Just don't overdo things."

"I hear that Otto and Grover and Sandy were placed on probation," continued Jose.

"That's it. They're supposed to find work. But I saw them around with Syd in their car earlier today."

"That is too bad for Syd," Jose suggested. "Is it not?"

"Syd's got his own way to go," returned Jack. He did not want to talk about his former friend. It made him angry, also unhappy, to see that little group of four riding about in Syd's car. The next time, he thought, Syd would be in the soup, along with his buddies.

"I will run some more," Jose announced. "My legs feel as though they did not belong to me."

He trotted off to the outfield. Jack saw Lion stalking and bent to scratch his head.

Coach Johnson came along and asked, "What do you think? Will Cansino be able to do it?"

"I'd say he'll make it. But you know that virus leaves you pretty weak."

"It worries me." Johnson looked harassed. "The Bells beat Cienega High 13 to 0 the other day."

"I read about it."

"Birkie looks fine. He should have won that game on Saturday. I wish I'd taken him out and used Tod, now. He was going so good I thought we might catch them. Then we needed his experience."

"But we didn't catch 'em," said Jack. "It was one of those things. I wish the guys wouldn't fret about it."

"You can't blame them." The coach was philosophical. "We were going great and we'd already beaten Bellingham—and then it fell apart. I only hope we can put it together again."

"Very few ball teams go undefeated," Jack pointed out.

"We almost made it." Johnson shrugged and walked away, intent on coaching Jay Byron on the cutoff play.

Lion turned and walked toward the fence adjoining Curzon Street. He had no particular purpose, just wanted the exercise. He kept in better shape than most athletes. It was part of his character to do so.

He saw the station wagon coming down the street, so perched on top of the fence, watching. Syd was driving. Sitting next to him was Otto. Lion's fur bristled. He hissed long and loud.

In the station wagon, Otto said, "There's that cat. Wish I had a rifle."

"Why blame the cat?" asked Syd. "He didn't put you up to a fool stunt like that, did he?"

"It had them all buffaloed," bragged Otto. "If the cat hadn't tipped them off, they'd never have known."

"So what?"

"You're not very friendly today," Otto complained. "Stop here awhile. I want to see the heroes after they blew the game to Woodland."

Syd told him, "If I stop here and you get caught, then what?"

"Go on. Drive on!" urged Grover. "We can't hang around school. They'll send us away."

"Chicken," jeered Otto. "You're all chicken. I'd have got away with it if you hadn't squealed."

Syd laughed. "Big man! They had that piece of cloth. They only needed to go to the laundry and ask if your pants were ever ripped like that and you were a dead pigeon. And anyway, why should Sandy and Grover take the rap when it was your idea?"

"They'd have sent us away if we didn't talk," Sandy agreed. "You've got no beef coming, Otto."

The big blond boy subsided. He had lost face, that was apparent. He had to do something to regain his imagined position. They were passing the Cansino house just then and he thought about the dog. "You know what? Some of the guys are saying they missed the big dog. You know? That if he'd been there, they would've won the game."

"That's a laugh. They blew it, that's all. If Syd had been playin' shortstop, they'd have won."

Syd said nothing, smarting beneath the skin.

Otto sat up straight. "Hey, that's an idea. If the dog means so much, how about they don't have it around for Saturday's game against the Bells?"

"Are you crazy?"

"No, I'm serious. Anyway, it'd be fun. We could kidnap the dog, hold him 'til after the game, then turn him loose."

"You're going to kidnap that dog? Why, you're scared to death of him," Syd said.

"Not any more. Not since I found out they're tame. Hey, that's an idea. I'm goin' to work on it."

"You are out of your skull," declared Grover.

Still, they were all silent, considering. They were angry at Jack Pilgrim and at Jose and at Aki; in fact, they were angry at the entire Studio City High School. If they could annoy or hamper the ball team, it would give them a feeling of revenge gained by their skill and brains.

They drove along, each with his own thoughts. Otto looked smug, slouched down in the seat, his feet on the dashboard.

......13........................

It was Junior's custom to sleep in his special oversize shelter until dawn, when a hundred bird voices broke on the morning air. Then he would rush out and cavort about the Cansino yard, playing games with his feathered friends. He never succeeded in catching one, but he was not disappointed, really, because once, in the country on a family picnic, he had caught a squawking chicken. It had not tasted very good and people seemed to be quite upset about the whole sorry business.

Still, running around among the twittering birds was all right. It helped get his day started. They didn't annoy him and he couldn't annoy them, so everything was fair and square.

On the Saturday morning of the game between the Green Sox and the Bells, Junior was up and at them as usual. He was, therefore, too preoccupied to notice when Grover came over the fence. He was at the far end of the yard when the intruder opened the gate and admitted Otto. The first thing he knew, there were two boys offering him goodies. He recognized the odor of hamburgers from the Drive-In Shoppe; Jose had procured them for him at times when the family was away—a feast for master and dog.

"Here, boy, good boy," one of the boys was saying in a shaky, nervous voice.

It was the same one who had played the odd game some time before, Junior remembered. Now he was grinning in a rather sickly manner and seemed ready to take flight at any instant. He had a friend with him, who was not scared, just a bit cautious. They both were casting quick glances at the house where the Cansino family slept. Junior could have told them no one would be up and around for hours, but he realized they did not speak his language.

He accepted one of the warm, greasy sandwiches, gobbling bun and meat in a gulp. Now they were going toward the gate with another succulent morsel extended. And the gate was open!

The Saint Bernard followed slowly. When he got to the gate, he saw the wooden station wagon and wrinkled his brow. The tall blond boy jumped a few feet, but the other said, "Come on, good boy, we go for a ride, huh?"

It was a moment of decision. The rear of the automobile was inviting. Junior could see inside clearly and know that there was plenty of room for even a Saint Bernard. These boys, whom he associated with Studio City High, had probably come early to take him to the game.

Jose had been busy all week, with scarcely time to give

any directions to the baseball team's mascot. Getting back his full strength had taken every moment of his time.

A second hamburger in the early dawn was a special treat. Junior truly appreciated small favors. And he liked boys—all boys. These did not seem to be members of the baseball team; at least, they had never been around when the games were being played, but Junior was not one to be fussy. They had food for him and they were friendly, excepting the blond, tall boy, who seemed timid.

Then he saw that the boy at the wheel was Syd Grimm, whom he remembered as a friend of Jack Pilgrim, who in turn, was Jose's *amigo*. Junior woofed once.

"*Shhh!* Come on, boy, get in the car," whispered the third boy. And wonder of wonders, this one had yet another hamburger!

They were certainly treating him like a king. He bounded around a moment, then jumped into the back of the car, drooling, his eyes bright. They closed it up behind him, but they had some kind of little light in there and the sandwich was just dandy. He munched this one, making it last a little longer, meanwhile eyeing the third, which was not withdrawn from him. His companions were willing to let him eat to his heart's content. They seemed like very nice boys.

After the third hamburger, Junior decided he would just take a nice nap. The floor of the auto was covered with some nice, soft stuff.

In the front seat of the station wagon, Otto said, "Listen to him. The dumb dog thinks he's among buddies."

"You'd better keep him thinking that way," warned Syd,

driving slowly along Curzon Street so that he might not attract undue attention. "You're sure this house is empty?"

"My uncle, who is a real estate dealer, is handlin' it for the owner," explained Otto, dangling a key. "This is a spare. We got it made, man."

"You sure do have a flock of uncles." Syd was not thoroughly convinced that Otto's elaborate plan was going to be entirely successful. "Is there water in the house?"

"Certainly there's water. I tell you, we can watch the game and be comfortable and keep the dog safely away—and nobody the wiser. When the game's over, we turn the dumb beast loose and he runs across the street and they think he got away, that's all. It's perfect, man."

"If anything goes wrong, you three will go away for a long trip," Syd warned him.

"You won't be so happy yourself," retorted Otto. "But nobody's goin' to catch us. I got it all figured out to the last detail, man."

"Stop calling me 'man,'" said Syd testily. "I thought we quit that jive talk."

"Man, like you're nervish today," hooted Otto. "Turn in here, in that driveway."

Syd drove in alongside a two-storied house across the street from the school baseball field. There was a garage in the rear. Otto opened the door and Syd drove inside. Then Otto closed the garage door, concealing the station wagon from view.

"Now we take the dog in the house with us," said Syd. "You leave him out here and he'll raise the neighborhood."

Otto objected. "Hey, we didn't figure on that."

"I thought you had everything planned? You just don't know anything about dogs."

"I don't like dogs."

"Then you shouldn't fool around with them." Syd was edgy. The whole thing seemed wrong to him.

He went around to the back of the car and opened the gate. Grover and Sandy came out, grinning.

"Hey, that's some mutt. He slept all the way. Look at him!"

Junior opened an eye. It had been a disappointing short ride. He stretched, rose and came down out of the car. The old friend of Jose and Jack patted his head, scratching between the ears where it felt so good. Everything was going well. It was just a question of time, now.

They all went through a side door, into the kitchen of the house. Their footsteps echoed. It was quite light now and they could see the empty rooms and the stairway leading up to the second floor. The boys had field glasses, borrowed from their families. Junior bounced ahead of them to the upper story. Otto had been right about the view.

There was a large front bedroom. From its windows a viewer could command the entire playing field. Adjusting their glasses, the boys scanned the deserted premises.

Otto exclaimed, "There's that cat! See it? Boy, I wish I had a gun!"

"You wouldn't shoot anything," Syd told him. "I wouldn't let you."

"I'd shoot that cat."

Syd said quietly, "Otto, sometimes I don't like you. This is one of those times."

"That cat got me in trouble."

"If I ever catch you hurting Lion, I'll beat your brains out," Syd warned. "Just remember that, Otto."

The blond boy flushed and started to reply. Then he looked at Syd's dark face and laughed a bit offkey. "Just kiddin', man, just kiddin'," he said.

Sandy interposed, "Gee, this is uncomfortable. I wish we had chairs, at least."

"There's some boxes in the garage," Grover remembered. "I'll get 'em."

"Bring up the food, too," said Sandy. "We got a long wait before the game begins."

"It'll be worth it," Otto insisted. "We got their mascot and we get to see them lose to the Bells. Nobody can tell us to stay away from the school!"

It was strange, Syd thought. They hated school. They quit the school. But they couldn't stay away from the school. There was something wrong with this way of thinking and acting. He looked through the glasses at Lion and had the queasy feeling that the cat was staring back at him.

As a matter of fact, that was precisely what Lion was doing. When the station wagon had turned into the driveway of the house across the street, Lion, atop the fence, had been in perfect position to see inside the car. It was impossible not to miss the sleeping bulk of Junior.

The whole business seemed strange to Lion. Why should the dog be across the street so early? It was an established custom for the dog to make his appearance with the baseball team as they came out on the field.

Were they going to have a parade across from that house? It could be; Lion was never quite able to figure out these matters. People and dogs were likely to try anything once. Cats minded their own business.

Also, it did seem odd that the boys who had set off the clamoring fire alarm and then tried to hide in that closet should be with Junior.

It was something Lion could investigate, as he had the hiding place at school.

When Jose Cansino opened his eyes that same morning, the sun was high. He jumped out of bed and went to the window, breathing deep, bending his knees. He felt in good shape again. He decided that he had completely recovered his condition, and was ready for the game this afternoon.

Then he thought of Junior. He had been neglecting the dog this week. There had been so many things to do—catching up on his class work, practicing with the team, making sure he got plenty of rest. He would spend the morning with the Saint Bernard, getting him ready for the big occasion of the game.

He showered and dressed and ran into the kitchen, where the bacon was giving off tempting odors. None of the family was on the scene. He heard voices in back and went out into the yard.

The moment he saw the open gate, he knew the worst.

Maria and Miguel were sniffling. Mama was wiping her eyes. Papa was out on the street, looking up and down.

Jose said, "Don't cry, anyone. Junior has done this before. He always comes back, yes?"

But he was worried as he joined his father.

Papa said, "I called him. I walked up and down and around the block, calling him."

"Can we go in the car to look?"

"But of course, after you've had your breakfast."

It was a difficult matter to eat. Everyone was too quiet. The family wondered if an outsider had opened the gate, which seemed strange. Papa went to the telephone and called the Humane Society and explained what had happened. He then called the police, with whom he was familiar because of his law practice, and asked their help. Still, they were all worried because of the game.

"It is not that the boys are superstitious," Papa explained to Mama. "It is that they are accustomed to having Junior with them by now. They play better knowing he is there at the bench."

"I realize you are right," said Mama. She motioned toward Jose. "It is he who worries me. He is too quiet, too contained. That is not normal."

"We will search," Papa promised.

Father and son got into the Cansino sedan and began to coast through the streets, stopping now and then to whistle in the way that was familiar to Junior.

As they drove up and down Curzon Street, they were observed from the upper window of the empty house. Otto was hugely pleased to see them looking for the dog.

It was Syd who had to keep Junior away from the window, which was just as well, since he was developing a deep distaste for this whole proceeding. He was not yet quite ready to admit it, but the whole setup seemed to lose glamour with every moment.

Otto called, "There's that finky Jack Pilgrim on his bicycle. Look at him! He's feeding the cat!"

Syd told them, "He always feeds Lion in the morning—even on Sunday."

"Now, that's a dopey thing to do, feed an old alley cat every morning. Imagine gettin' up early to feed a cat."

"Lion's not an alley cat; he's the school cat," Syd objected. "There's a difference."

"Man, you sure are dopey yourself today," said Otto. They're gone, now. You can let that old dog loose."

Syd returned to the front room and adjusted his field glasses. There was Jack, all right, with a paper package of food, and Lion was eating away, his tail erect with pleasure. Then Jack was going toward the gym. Coach Johnson was already there; his car could be seen parked in the lot. The pair would be poring over the line-ups and making plans to meet Bellingham.

Otto was going on, "The way I figure it, we got that greaser kid upset. No matter about the rest of 'em, the shortstop won't play his game."

"He was sick this week," Syd said.

"Yeah, how about that, man?" Otto was delighted.

Syd remembered when he had owned a terrier and it had run away. He had felt terrible for a long while. They never did find him . . . his name was Pike. He had missed that dog. He instinctively patted Junior's head and was rewarded by a floor thumping of the plumelike tail.

Time dragged by for the four boys in the vacant house. They drank soda pop and ate all the sandwiches and cake with which they had provided themselves. They did not forget to feed Junior, feeling that this would keep him quiet. It seemed years before there was activity on the ball field.

The Cansino car pulled up and Jose got out. His father said something to him and the boy nodded, trying to smile, Syd could see through the field glasses. Then the sedan drew away and Jose's shoulders slumped. He looked up and down the street, braced himself and entered the school ball field, walking slowly across toward the gym. Lion came from under the stands and accompanied him.

Syd took the glasses down from his eyes and blinked at Junior. The big dog was lying in a corner, sleeping. His stomach was full and he would not wake up for a while, Syd thought. Otto and the others were animated, watching the fans arrive, chortling over Jose's discomfort. The Bellingham team appeared in a bus which drove in to the door of the dressing room. The umpires came in their blue suits and black shoes. Syd was restless and unhappy.

Down in the Green Sox locker room there was more unhappiness. Jose answered a dozen questions, long of face, helpless to explain Junior's disappearance. Coach Johnson called a friend of his in the Sheriff's department, asking them to co-operate in finding Junior.

Jack Pilgrim was utterly distressed. "But who could

have opened the gate? You didn't see any of that bunch around, did you? Otto and those guys?"

"No, we saw no one. It must have been very early in the morning when he got out. And the gate was open once before."

"It's a rotten deal," Jack declared. "We've got trouble enough with the Bells."

"Trouble indeed," said Jose. He felt lost as he put on his uniform. Yet he knew he had to perform at his best. He gritted his teeth, forcing his worriment to the back of his mind.

He went through all the preliminaries to the contest with his teeth shut tight. He forced himself not to look over his shoulder at the gate. If Junior did come to the field, he would know it at once by the uproar, he told himself. The stands were full of people who had by now heard the bad news.

The Bellingham team looked as big and as expert as before. They had not changed their line-up, they were satisfied that the championship was theirs if they stood pat with their stars.

Coach Johnson made only two small changes: batting Hatfield second and dropping long-ball hitter Sampson to third spot. Then he had moved Aki Matsuo up to seventh in the order so that Barker might lend strength in the eighth position. Birkie would start the game on the mound. Tod would be warming up in case of disaster.

Jossman looked bigger than ever and just as cool and collected, exercising easily in the Bells warmup spot. He certainly had that overpowering speed, Jose knew. It was going to be a tight ballgame, he thought as he took the field, picked up a pebble, and returned the infield tosses to Keel at first.

Al Birkie sauntered to the pitcher's box and faced Keller. He looked around at his teammates, nodded, and went to work. He threw the slider, the slow curve, the change-up, nothing too fast, moving the ball around.

On a three and two count Keller banged one and it came winging down to short, a hard chance, one which had to be charged. Jose trapped it and made his throw. The first of the Bellingham hitters was out at first.

Now it was Ober. He swung valiantly at one of Birkie's junk pitches. It ascended to the sky and Jose dashed in calling, "Mine! Mine!"

Birkie had to step aside as Jose caught it almost on the pitcher's mound. He grinned and said, "That's right, I throw 'em, you catch 'em."

"Two down, one to go," Jose reminded him. "Let's go." He was wrapped deep in the game now, all else forgotten.

Carney, always dangerous, waved a bat. Jose moved, giving a little room, since he was able to pull the ball.

Carney fooled him. He hit into the hold exposed to Jose's right. It was necessary to take a skip and a hop and make his throw without setting himself.

Harry Keel stretched, reached out, trapped the ball. The Bells had gone down in order and the pitchers' battle was on. Jossman might be overpowering, but Birkie was canny. It seemed a good match.

Jose selected his heavy bat and went to the plate. Jossman stretched his long arms and sought his sign from Einstein, the catcher.

Jose crouched. The ball came in like a meteor.

"Stuh—rike!"

Could it be possible Jossman had more speed than ever? Jose could believe it. The ball seemed harder to follow as it left the tall hurler's hand.

Next came a curve. Jose followed it, snapped his wrists. The impact stung his hands. He ran hard. Everly grabbed the grounder, threw underhand to Sykes at first. Jose was out.

Jossman merely grunted, faced Chris Hatfield, wound up, exercised his long arm. Hatfield swung and went all the way around, missing. He went the same way on two more and was a strikeout victim.

Sampson went up with fire in his eye. The fire may have got in the way of his judgment. He also went down by the kayo route.

It was back to work on the field. Sykes, the lank first baseman, led off. He picked on a slider and blooped it into center. Jack made a great run but had to trap it, and the Bells had their first hit.

As the stands howled, Jose called, "Let them hit it, Birkie. That's the way to go, let 'em hit. We got 'em."

Birkie, always calm, pitched to Anthony, the third baseman. It was a curve. Anthony picked on it, banging hard. The ball flashed down to Aki, who fielded it, swung and snapped a throw to second.

Jose was there. Sykes barreled in, but Jose had learned to avoid those sliding blocks. He jumped and overhanded to Keel. The ball beat the runner by a step and suddenly there were two out, nobody on.

Birkie grinned and said, "You told 'em, Jose. They hit 'em, you field 'em."

He pitched to Toler. On two and two, he eased one of his sneaky fast balls across the inside corner for a third strike to retire the side.

Jack Pilgrim led off the second. Jose sat on the end of the bench and could not refrain from thinking, suddenly and acutely, of Junior, whose place was there beside him. He bit his lip and turned strict attention upon Jossman, straining to catch one little move which might betray the pitches the Bells hurler was throwing.

Jack swung, nailed the ball on the nose. It went like an arrow . . . straight to Ober in right field for the out.

Keel was next and he also caught one on the good wood of the bat. Eberly was in front of this one, to throw out Keel at first.

Nick Farmer strove mightily, fouling off five or six, then got fooled on the change-up and was called out.

Jose arose thoughtfully. The curve ball, he speculated, it was just barely possible that Jossman was hesitating a split second before delivering it. This could be wrong, but Jose tucked it away in his mind for future reference.

The game settled down to the pitchers' battle Jose had expected would take place. Birkie had found his maturity and Jossman was . . . Jossman.

The next time Jose was at bat he tried to use the knowledge he had gained by watching. He guessed completely wrong on one pitch, looked foolish swinging late on the swift. The next time he waited too long. Then he struck out.

In the seventh he had another chance. This time he got hold of the ball. It seemed to be going through for a hit when Eberly made a great play and throw to nail him.

Jossman had not given up a hit. Indeed, not a Studio City player had reached first base through the seventh.

Birkie had walked only one man and had given up the single in the second. Jose had been ever so correct, it was a tight ball game.

Lion deserted his spot high in the stands. He came down slowly, tail erect, and moved to the Green Sox bench. He seemed to sense that things were not going too well.

Jack scratched the cat's ears and said, "We're kind of lost without our mascot, your friend, Junior. Why don't you bring him back, old man?"

Lion meowed and watched his friend run out on the field. He knew it was not right that the big dog should be across the street and not here, where he belonged. Lion rather missed the Saint Bernard.

Birkie had been working very hard. As the eighth inning began, he took more time than usual. The sun was hot and he was not a burly boy. He may have been tired before then, but now Jose thought he could detect weariness in the game Green Sox pitcher. Sykes, first baseman of the visitors, was leadoff man.

Birkie's curve ball hung a little. Sykes punched at it. Jose scuttled to his left and flung himself on the ground, stretching. The ball hit his glove and dribbled into the outfield. By the time Jose retrieved it, Sykes was on first.

Birkie took a deep breath. Anthony, the next hitter, had always been easy for him, but somehow the payoff throw missed the plate and the third-sacker walked.

Now it was Toler, a canny batsman. Birkie tightened his belt, inhaled deeply and threw all he had into a curve.

As though he had been waiting all day just for that pitch, Toler came around. He knocked it over Aki's head.

Sykes scooted, never hesitated at third, running like a wild creature for home. Jack Pilgrim tried to cut him down. Barker put the ball on him, but Sykes was safe and the first run of the game was in ... for Bellingham.

Coach Johnson motioned to Tod Hunter. Then he walked out onto the field. Birkie, he realized, was worn out.

Silence struck the Studio City fans. Lion became uneasy, staring, then moving. He strolled with dignity toward the far-off fence. The boys needed cheering and the big dope seemed able to do something for them. It was worth a try.

Birkie was handing the ball to the Coach. "I was expecting you. Seems like it won't go where I want it to go. Sorry."

The infield gathered around. They all had words of real praise and condolence for the dead-game southpaw. Roly-poly Tod came walking from behind the stands where he had been getting his arm warmed up.

Birkie left and Tod began taking his pitches, slow and easy.

Across the street in the upstairs room Otto was jubilant. "The Bells finally cracked through. That's it for Studio City, men. Jossman's too much . . . too much!"

Syd strained his eyes through the field glasses. It seemed all too true. The championship was slipping away. He should be happy about it . . . yet, somehow, he was not. He looked at Junior, who was just waking from his long sleep. Something inside Syd Grimm turned over. It was as though he and the dog had awakened at the same moment.

Half to himself, Syd announced, "This is plain crazy."

Otto wheeled away from the window, glowering. "What was that jazz, man?"

"Don't call me 'man' again. And I say this is just like that dumb stunt you pulled with the fire alarm."

"Cut it, Syd, cut it," Otto cautioned. "We're winning the ball game, that's what counts."

"You're plain stupid. You don't know anything about dogs and you don't know anything about baseball, either."

Syd felt as though a huge tight spring inside him had begun to unwind. The other two boys were staring at him.

Otto said, "You've been on my back all day!"

Syd's hand was on Junior's ruff. It gave him confidence. "I'm going to take this dog and walk across the street with him. You can take off, all of you. I don't care where you go; just don't get in touch with me."

"You're going to do what?"

"The sensible thing," said Syd. "Come on, Junior."

He started for the door. Junior hesitated, then lumbered after him.

Otto cried, "Get him, men!"

They all came at once, fearful now that somehow they would be caught and sent to reform school. Syd ducked the first rush and got his back to the wall.

"You may get me," he warned them, "but it'll cost you before you're through."

They encircled him. He was the strongest of them and the only real athlete. There was no chance of his escaping all three, but none wanted to be the first to go in. Otto danced around, exhorting his cronies, but making no effort to charge.

Junior, the most nonviolent of creatures, thought it was part of a game. He did not like the belligerent sound of their voices, but some boys played rough, he knew. He made a couple of sportive passes and found himself ignored. He sat down to think it over. He wished Jose were here.

Meanwhile, downstairs, Lion had found a window open a crack. It did not seem possible that he could squeeze his husky frame through the narrow space, but he measured it with the spread of his whiskers and began to wriggle his way inside.

There was the sound of scuffling upstairs. Lion worked harder, left some fur behind, dropped to the floor. Unlike Junior, he was an animal that had no aversion to a fight. He had not kept the school grounds clear of intruders for eight years without a spirit of combat. He flew up the steps.

Syd was in the grip of Sandy and Grover. They had grabbed him as he made a break for freedom. Grover's fist glanced across his eye. Junior was hovering, beginning to wonder if this really was a game and if he shouldn't take an active part in it.

Lion let out his warrior's cry and dove right into the thick of it. He was scratching and biting and hissing all at the same time. He recognized his enemies of the fire alarm episode and clawed into them like a bobcat.

The sudden attack threw Sandy off balance as a claw hooked his ankle. He yelled, falling back. Syd used that moment to spin Grover and throw him into Otto. Junior put himself in the way of the trio as Lion continued to fill the air with challenging yowls.

Syd called, "Remember, I won't squeal on you. Just get lost, all three of you."

He went plunging down the stairs, with Junior at his heels. Lion remained long enough to extend a last token of the meeting, then flew past his enemies and down the stairs.

Syd, Junior and Lion went out the side door and walked across Curzon Street together, the animals moving more proudly than the boy.

When they entered the gate, and the crowd caught sight of them, there was a yell which shook the ground. The cheer leaders began tumbling and howling, and the spectators in the stands started whooping. Syd knew he was going to have a lot of explanations to make, but he felt better than he had in months, in fact, since he had been expelled from the baseball squad. He felt as though he had just taken a good, long, invigorating shower-bath.

Jack Pilgrim came running over. Tod had just finished his warmup. Syd realized things had happened suddenly in the room across the street. The game was about to resume.

"Where in the world did you come from?" demanded Jack.

"I'll tell you later," Syd responded.

"Hey, you've got an eye on you!"

"Somebody hit me." Syd shook his head. He shouldn't have said that if he wanted to protect Otto and the others. "Never mind. Forget it," he urged.

He went on toward the bench. Jose ran over from his shortstop position and threw an arm around Junior's neck.

"Bad dog, running away!" he cried, laughing, hugging hard to show he did not mean the reprimand.

"He didn't run; he was taken," Syd explained.

"So long as he is here," Jose said. "Thank you, Syd. Thank you very much."

He went back on the field. Syd moved toward Coach Johnson, who was coming with the leash. Sooner or later, he would have to tell the story to the Coach and to everyone, Syd knew. Meantime, it was a joyous occasion for all of Studio City.

"Come and sit on the bench," offered Coach Johnson.

"No, thanks. I'll just go into the stands." Syd walked

quickly away, evading those who would praise him for returning the mascot. He sat alone, silent, his eyes on the ball field where the Green Sox were a run behind with men on the bases for the Bells.

Jose was back in the ball game, dancing around, imbued with new zest. Tod Hunter finished warming up and stared at Eberly, all the easy good nature gone from him. The Bells were supposed to be fast-ball hitters . . . and that was all Tod had—good speed and control.

Junior, among his friends at last, let out one long, happy sigh, then settled down beside Coach Johnson. Lion half-closed his eyes, satisfied thus far with events.

Tod threw a look at the bench, at Junior. Then he reached back and zoomed the ball at the plate.

Eberly swung. He was far too late. Tod had found extra speed, the ball looked like a cold tablet going into Barker's mitt.

A moment later Eberly was walking away, shaking his head in bewilderment. Einstein took his place and Tod kept right on throwing the only way he knew, harder and quicker. Einstein whiffed.

Jossman was next. He was easy.

Tod had retired the side in nine pitches.

But Jossman was still the hero on the mound. Jack Pilgrim hit one a mile, but too high. Ober in right field accepted it. Keel struck out. Farmer fouled out.

Nothing daunted, Tod went back to his job. The top of the Bells batting order looked just the same as the bottom to him. He got them in prompt order.

So now it was the last half of the last inning with Studio

City one run behind and Jossman still going like a steam engine. Aki was the first man to bat. Coach Johnson looked up and down the bench, but there was no one to pinch-hit who was any better risk than the little second baseman.

Aki paused where Jose sat beside Junior. "I'll get on. One way or another, I'll get on."

"You got to." The strain was terrible. Jose gripped Junior's ear until the dog squealed and licked at his hand.

Aki adjusted his safety helmet and went to the plate, glaring at Jossman, his nemesis. He let a strike go by, then a ball, crowding, waving his bat.

Jose was watching every pitch. He still believed he had caught something, a tiny move to tip the curve. Now, he thought, Jossman would come in with a swift one to jam Aki and send him away from the plate. Then he would throw that nickel curve, that fast slider, which fooled Aki every time.

Sure enough, there went the inside pitch. Aki fell away from it. But it seemed to Jose that the second-sacker did not try to fall too quickly as he turned his head. The ball glanced off his helmet, he lay there, stunned for the moment.

But when Coach Johnson got to him he was on his feet, grinning from ear to ear. He wobbled down to first, waving them aside, then staggered a step.

"Byron . . . Run for Matsuo," ordered Coach Johnson.

Aki came to the bench, still grinning, and whispered to Jose, "You see? I did it."

"You might've been killed."

"I had to get on. Maybe I couldn't have ducked it, anyway. Who knows?"

Fred Barker, gripping his bat, was at the plate. Jossman glowered at Byron on first, kneading a ball as though to tear it apart. Jose moved to the bat rack as Junior whinnied.

Coach Johnson said, "We play to tie, understand?"

"Yes, sir," replied Jose.

He watched Barker lay down a fine bunt. Jossman had to go to first as Byron easily took second.

Jack Pilgrim joined the Coach and Jose and observed, "It's going to be up to you, amigo."

"As you say." Jose was taut but oddly not nervous. He was thinking hard. Tod Hunter struck out. Two away and a man on second. A hit was needed to keep the Green Sox alive in this championship game.

Jossman was rocklike. Jose went up and stood there, his heavy bat poised. Jossman jammed him good for the first strike.

Jose tapped dirt from his spikes and settled in. The Bells' pitcher reared back, came over and down. Again it was a clean strike.

Now Jossman could waste a couple. He threw the change-up and a curve, both wide. With the count even, Jose did not stir, nor did he take his eyes from Jossman's pitching arm.

Jossman stretched, checked Jay, threw. This time Jose thought he detected that hesitation, the flick of the wrist which meant the slider was coming. He held the bat at the end, flat-footed for once. He eagerly followed the streaking ball. He saw it break.

He brought the big stick around with everything, all the strength in his slender body. There was a loud and satisfactory booming sound.

Syd Grimm came to his feet and found himself howling through trumpeted hands, "Run, little guy, run!"

Junior was barking at the top of his range as out in right field Ober gave chase. From center field, Keller joined, running out from under his cap.

The ball fell between them. It rolled toward the fence.

Byron came prancing in, waving his arms, turning to urge Jose onward. Jack Pilgrim clenched his fists as though to drag the shortstop around the bases.

Jose hit third. They tried to stop him, to play for the tie with none out. Jose had glanced over his shoulder; he did not see the baseline coach. He only saw Ober ready to throw . . . in deep, deep center. He put down his head and sprinted.

Einstein had the plate blocked. He leaned forward for the bounce of the ball. Jose left his feet. He hit the dirt in a blockbuster of a lightning slide. At the last moment he hooked. He went around the catcher. His foot slapped gainst the rubber.

"Yer safe!" bawled the umpire.

The ball game was over, the championship won. It had been saved by the intelligent use of good eyesight, by good judgment, by co-ordination and a loyal heart that would function with or without the help of a mascot and devoted friend named Junior, thought Coach Johnson. It had been saved by stout hearts and willing hands.

The fans descended like locusts and picked Jose up on their shoulders. Jack Pilgrim gave them a hand. They paraded around the bases, singing the victory song. Aki found himself hoisted, and then all of them, all the nine plus Jay Byron and Birkie.

Jossman waited, a good sport. He extended a huge hand and asked, "How'd you do it, Cansino?"

"Since you are graduating, I'll tell you," Jose answered. "You tip your curve ball," Jose told him, grinning. "I wish you luck in college."

"Thanks," said the Bells pitcher. "Thanks a whole lot. You guys have really got it . . . here." He tapped the left side of his chest and vanished in the crowd.

Junior was demanding attention. Jose put his fist on the dog's furry neck and they ran for the dressing room.

Syd Grimm was waiting there. He faced the entire team as they piled in, full of glee and laughter. After a moment they fell silent, sensing that something of importance was about to take place. Coach Johnson entered, and Syd put his back against a locker.

"Something, Syd?" asked the Coach.

"About Junior. You might as well know now as later. I thought it would be a cute idea to dognap him."

"You thought what?" Coach Johnson's neck turned red.

"Yes, sir. I admit it and I'm ready to take my punishment."

Jack Pilgrim said, "You stole Junior, then you brought him back? Why bring him back?"

Chuck Johnson swallowed hard and nodded. "I'd like to know the answer to that one, Syd."

"And who hit you in the eye? It's a pretty blue and red," Jack pointed out.

"I ran into some interference."

Coach Johnson said, "I'll bet you did."

"Look, I'm guilty, that's all. It was a dumb stunt." Syd gulped and turned away.

Jack said, "Wait a minute. Let's ask Jose about this."

As Jose went forward from the corner where he and Junior were having a lively reunion, Lion came stalking through the doorway. Syd just stood still, unable to say anything more.

Lion coiled around Syd's feet and purred like the motor of an ancient jeep. Junior galumphed up to him and leaned against him adoringly, woofing gently, rubbing hard.

Jose said, "Junior often runs away. I do not know anything about dognaping."

"Yes," said Jack, "if you don't know anything about whoever gave you that black eye, Syd, why should we believe your story about a stolen dog? What do you say, Coach?"

Chuck Johnson was a wise man. He could sense the way the other boys felt about the affair, too, and he knew that it was best to cement relationships among them.

"Let's put it this way," he said. "If you, Syd, can forget the past, so can we. Let's talk about the future."

"Yes, sir," Syd told him. "I want to stay in school. I found out what it means to drop out. I was listening to the wrong people. I know it now—and maybe we can make them realize how things actually are, too."

"That's good enough for me." The Coach started for his office.

"One more thing, sir, please," Syd went on.

"Yes?"

"The owner of the dog, Jose. I owe him and Aki an apology."

"No," said Jose, "the past, it is forgotten."

"That is correct," Aki agreed.

Jack Pilgrim stepped briskly forward from his locker. "Supposing you all shake hands and let's get over this serious business. We just won the Conference championship!"

Tod Hunter exclaimed, "Whee! Ice cream and cake tonight!"

The celebration began again, on a high note.

Junior joined in, enjoying every moment of it. He cavorted and jumped and woofed and licked the faces of one and all, whenever he saw an unguarded opening.

Lion remained on the outskirts. Jack petted him, and so did Syd, who was grateful for his fighting sortie. That was all right with the cat, but when the boys began throwing water and snapping wet towels, he established an observation post for himself on top of the lockers. That kind of nonsense was all right for a dog, but it did not agree with him. After all, an eight-year-old feline with the responsibility of conducting an entire school—grounds, building and people—had to maintain a certain superiority.

WILLIAM R. COX

was born and educated in New Jersey. He worked on Newark newspapers as a sports reporter and feature writer, always attempting to create fiction until he finally broke into the magazine field, in the days when there were hundreds of periodicals publishing short stories. He produced over a thousand such tales before turning to the new era of television and paperbacks.

He has written twenty-four books, including several sports yarns for Dodd, Mead. He works in television and motion pictures upon occasion, always returning to his first and lasting love, the printed word.

William Cox's hobbies, oddly enough, are reading and writing. He does watch professional sports—live and on television. He dwells in California, among tomato plants from Jersey, Satsuma plums, avocados, smog—and scenarios.